CEDAR KEY STORIES

Island Interludes

Gary Wadley

CEDAR KEY STORIES

The characters and events portrayed in this book are fictitious. Any similarity to real persons, living or dead, is coincidental and not intended by the author.

No part of this book may be reproduced, or stored in a retrieval system, or transmitted in any form or by any means, electronic, mechanical, photocopying, recording, or otherwise, without express written permission of the publisher and author.

Gills and *The Rest of the World* originally appeared in:
Academy Arts Press 2019 Short Story Anthology

Cover design and photo by: Gary Wadley

Printed in the United States of America

Copyright © 2020 Gary Wadley

All rights reserved. (6)

Photos and drawings by the author, except

"WWW with castnet" photo courtesy of Milinda Allen

"Beautiful Dreamer" lyrics by Stephen Foster

ISBN-13:978-1718-1636-69

WinterClock Press

DEDICATION

*For Sweet Vicky,
Annie, Emily, Katie, Ben,
and Cedar Key Sharks Everywhere*

CONTENTS

Preface	6
The Rest of the World	9
Battle of Number Four	17
Gills	23
Catbirth	39
Pictures of Jesus	46
Two Hearts	51
The Dear	54
A Short History of Cedar Key	67
How to Catch a Shark	72
Mist	84
The Honey Dipper	88
Uncle Tyre	94
Shorty	103
The Red Violin	108
The Tree of Life	117
The Oyster Egg	126
The Pisshead	132
Eating Christmas	138
Starship	144
Rousing the Turtle	148
Bonus Story	154
Epilogue	156
Map of Cedar Key	158

"Just 'cause you can't see somethin' don't mean it ain't there."
- Margaret (Resident of Cedar Key)

But God hath chosen the foolish things of the world to confound the wise; and God hath chosen the weak things of the world to confound the things which are mighty; and base things of the world, and things which are despised, hath God chosen, yea, and things which are not, to bring to naught things that are: <u>that</u> no flesh should glory in his presence.
- I Corinthians 1:27-29 (KJV)

"There are more things in heaven and earth, Horatio, than are dreamt of in your philosophy."
- Hamlet to Horatio

PREFACE

This is a set of stories about Cedar Key - past, present, and future. Cedar Key is a real place where time is different. You'll know you are in Cedar Key when you are there. Time is measured by tide, and forgotten altogether by horseshoe crabs. The sweet breeze brings memories, and angry storms wash them away. There are clamshell graves, wizened trees, and pelicans posing on posts and bobbing on waves. Fiddler crabs wave on the beach and sleepy cats yawn on sunny porches. Most of the year you'll need bug spray. It is far from The Mouse.

On the way to Cedar Key (if you drive) you will pass Rosewood. There is a historical marker but you might miss it. Some folks were killed there because of their skin color. Part of one of the stories takes place there.

As of this writing, there are no stoplights or fast food restaurants, and there never have been. They screwed the place up some when they built a road on the beach in the name of progre$$. The sewer system is much better than it used to be when it was a pipe that ran poop straight into the gulf at the bottom of 4th Street. The folks that live in Cedar Key are transplants, natives, and in-betweens, and are like everyone else . . . only more so (much like relatives).

If you don't want to drive, Cedar Key has a little airport, and folks fly in for good seafood and a visit. Be careful, though: sometimes pilots lose the horizon and crash because the sky and sea blend together. Never lose the horizon. It's easy to do.

As you cross the first little bridge (another story occurs there – the site of an actual Civil War battle) you'll notice a blend of salt and marsh, of fecund life and muddy decay. You will see all manner of birds, waiting and watching, jousting for fish or flying in congress. Unlike Congress, *they* know where they are going. Be aware there are many things on the water and under the water and on the land, pretty things and nice things and dangerous things. In these stories some of them speak.

And there are memories, even if you've never been there.

One more thing: there is an ancient piece of machinery a little out from shore at 4th and G Streets. Some say it's a remnant of the old 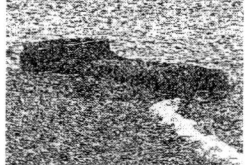 cedar mill and some say it's part of the boiler from an old steamship. Actually, it has been there at least a million years and is part of a starship. Such things happen. Remember – time is different in Cedar Key.

If you like these stories you can drop some coins in the box part of the rusted thing. Every now and then some city official might collect the change and give it to the Women's Club or some other worthy cause. In any case, watch out for sting rays.

One more one more thing: not all of the islands are visible - not to everyone anyway.

These stories are fictitious and represent no actual person or thing -- unless you think they do. If you do, tell them (or it) I said hello. Certain liberties have been taken.

The photos and drawings are mostly my own.

P.S. The pink-tailed Cedar Key skink really lives there, though it is endangered and might be extinct by the time you read this - an extinct skink. How sad.

P.P.S. *The Tree of Life* story was actually written by one of the characters in the book. Many thanks to her for letting me use it.

Don't lose your horizon.

End of The Runway – Cedar Key

THE REST OF THE WORLD

Leo saw it when he went to make his morning coffee - a little fiddler crab in the kitchen sink, standing on the scratched porcelain, waving its one fat claw like a truce flag. He studied it a moment, then filled the percolator with water and coffee and placed it on the gas stove, which let out a soft fart when he turned on the gas.

The crab was still there when the coffee began to percolate, though it had moved a few inches and seemed to be picking at a piece of scrap in the sink. Leo thought the crab might go back down the sink drainpipe that led under the house to the beach, to the gulf, to the rest of the world. *The screen at the end of the drain has come off*, Leo thought, perhaps aloud.

Leo lived alone and conversed with himself, with the animate and the inanimate, no longer caring to distinguish between the two. After the passing of his wife he decided it made no difference. He would talk to a chair or a rock as readily as to a bird or cat. Speaking to things comforted him as one is comforted by holding a smashed finger or rubbing a bumped head, so it was nothing that he should speak to the little crab.

"You should go home," he said, though he really didn't mind the visiting crab. Not long ago he would have gently picked up the creature (avoiding its one big claw) and carried it out of the house, back to the beach, but he was old now and tired and inclined to let things do as they wanted. He remembered how, when he was a boy, the fiddlers would swarm over the beach at low tide, colorful in the sun as they emerged from their little holes in the sand. He figured they must be eating and courting, the males impressing the females with their one big claw, but always in the end the tide returned and they retreated to their burrows to be covered by the water. It delighted him that a crab could live underwater and in the air at the same time.

When the coffee was ready, Leo sat at the scarred dining table and thought about his day. He knew weather was coming because his knees and shoulders ached. He did not mind weather so much now because he no longer worked on the water and was content to watch through his front window whatever blew in from the gulf. He did not care for the light of the sun, because as it broke on the water it blinded one; and after a while the eyes got milky, and sometimes sores that would not heal bloomed on the arms and nose. When he thought of this he was sad for those who must go out on the water.

He heard scratching in the sink and remembered the fiddler. Perhaps he would make the effort to put him in a mug and free him on the beach at low tide.

There was a knock on the door. Then another knock and someone called his name; it was the woman from the government, come to bother him again. He knew if he did not answer she would try all the doors and eventually return and threaten to put him in a home, so he went to the door.

The government woman was a Miss Claudia Brown. Leo didn't actually know if she was a Miss, though he couldn't see how a woman like her could be anything else. Her thick body was topped by a broad and sad face that itself was topped by an arrangement of grey hair. Her hair reminded Leo of seagulls fighting over a scrap of fish. A government worker, she exuded a self-important and efficient uselessness.

Leo opened the door, then retreated quickly as Miss Brown charged inside. He was raised to be polite and said nothing.

"Leo," she said. He could not tell if it was a question or a statement and looked at her as though she were a strange chair that had turned up in his house.

"Leo," she said again, "As you know, we're worried about you, that you're not getting enough to eat, that you're all alone. What if we --"

"I eat government cheese," he said. "Those big bricks last a long time." Leo had learned that the word "we" was seldom used for his benefit.

She shook her head, sent seagulls flying. "Yes, but – what?" Miss Brown heard a faint scratching sound and turned toward the noise. "You have company?" she asked. Leo never had company.

"And I have a friend now." He nodded toward the kitchen. He wanted to tell her it was really none of her business, but knew that would only encourage the government-sanctioned part of her, so he said, simply, "Yes. I have a visitor in the kitchen sink." There were times he envied those naughty boys who could emit gas at will.

Miss Brown looked at him, showing large teeth. "The sink?" She asked this as though she might have discovered a way to untie a difficult knot.

Leo nodded and she walked into the kitchen uninvited, as a cat upon a bird, slow, focused. "The sink?" she repeated. The little crab was still there and stopped scratching as soon as the government worker's huge face rose over the rim of the sink. The creature tilted his eye stalks back and stared at her, then began to wave its large claw. "Hello," it said.

Of course, Claudia Brown reasoned she did not hear what she heard. Crabs do not speak: the floor joint had creaked, or Leo had made a sound in the other room. Crabs, even intelligent ones (if there were such a thing) had no speaking apparatus. The only thing Claudia had seen come from a crab's mouth was bubbles – she'd eaten enough crab to know there was no tongue, no lips, no speech.

"How...?" she asked, not the crab, but Leo, who had remained at the front door.

"How what?" he said.

Miss Brown stood for a moment looking around the kitchen, then down to the little crab that was busy with something in the sink. She cleared her throat, then spun and left the house, leaving a pleasantly empty space.

After a moment Leo entered the kitchen and said, "What happened? What did you do?"

"Nothing. I just said, 'Hello'," said the crab.

Leo nodded, amazed at the power of simple words.

Claudia Brown sat with Vince Gooden in the Redundant Café, a small place in Gainesville where they met when privacy was required, where it was unlikely anyone from Cedar Key would see them. Claudia liked to imagine they met there because it was intimate. Vince was *the* developer in Levy County and her very special friend. Their arrangement had been financially and personally beneficial and she was excited about the news she was about to deliver. She blew on her coffee and said, "He's crazy and it won't be long before he's gone."

"How long?" Vince asked. He knew there were no relatives, no third-party claims on the house. With Leo gone, he would purchase the waterfront house at auction, remodel, and sell for a fortune.

"That depends," Claudia said. "He's definitely senile." She paused and smiled at Vince, pleased at her own cleverness. "He keeps a fiddler crab as a pet in his sink – even talks to it." It was only a little lie. She did not mention it was the crab that talked. "I need to do a few more observations, document another episode of nuttiness, then we'll petition for a hearing. He'll be found incompetent, made a ward of the state and moved to a home."

Vince drew a cigarette from a pack and tapped it on the table as he looked at Claudia. So homely, he thought, but useful; and beachfront property was . . . he felt Claudia's leg brush against his under the table and he lit the cigarette, blowing a smoke cloud over her head.

Leo and the crab became friends (as much as one can become friends with a crab): the man was grateful the little creature had scared away the government woman and did not mind conversation; the crab (so he said) was grateful for the scraps of food the man left in the sink. Leo did not fix the screen over the drainage pipe. After a few days, the man carefully placed the little creature on a plate at his table so that they could talk more comfortably. He gathered a bit of seaweed and a little sand from the beach and put it on the plate so that the crab would feel at home. Some evenings they talked for hours, the man leaning close so that his friend would not have to strain his small voice.

"You are hard on the outside and soft on the inside," Leo would say.

The crab would then tap the plate with his claw as though making a toast and say, "And you are soft on the outside and hard on the inside."

Leo grinned and was not surprised the crab knew this because crabs eat many things as they go about cleaning up the waters. He himself had gained a bit of knowledge from eating blue crabs and stone crabs when he could get them. He boiled them until they reddened like the evening sun and cracked them open to get at the succulent meat and juices. He did not mention this to the little crab, of course. All in all, he was glad for the company, and though it occurred to him that he might be crazy, surely there was no harm in talking to a fiddler crab. Still, the crab talked back, and this made him wonder about the nature of his madness. In any case, he was careful to bathe at least a twice a week and he brushed his teeth every night, so he reasoned he wasn't too far gone.

One evening Leo read the crab an official looking letter he'd received, then set it down quickly, as if it might burst into flame.

"You have been very kind to me," said the crab. "Men don't like us much, probably because of our cousins the spiders -- though on the whole, spiders are not so bad." Leo liked spiders and took pains to place them outside if he found them wandering around the house -- even the black widow, who could not help how she was born. "I think," the crab said, "that I will help you -- that the next visit from the government lady should be at nine p.m. on the night of the fourteenth."

Leo was surprised that a crab should know of dates and times, but he reasoned that wild things probably knew a great deal about such things -- time and season and tide and sun and moon -- for that is how they lived; but to place a time and number upon a day impressed him greatly and he realized he still had much to learn.

"Why?" he asked.

The crab shrugged, though of course this was impossible. "It will be a full moon and . . ." The little eye stalks looked up to the man and seemed to blink, waiting.

"It will be low tide," said the man.

"Precisely," said the crab. "A very low tide -- You must tell the government lady that you have decided she is right – but that you wish to have a celebration before you leave your house."

"A celebration?"

"Certainly. The night of the fourteenth, to commence at nine p.m." The little crab began flicking sand across his plate. Leo nodded. "And," the crab continued, "you will invite only the government lady. No one else." Then the crab explained to him what he must do.

Claudia Brown was surprised to find an envelope wedged between her screen door and its frame. She was even more surprised that it was from Leo (she did not think he could write). She read:

Miss Brown You are rite. Its time. In celebrashun I invite you to a goinaway party at my hous on the fourteen of March at exatly nine p.m. You will be the speshal guest. Leo

She immediately called Vince Gooden to tell him the news; he told her she must go and then invited her over to his condo to celebrate. It became a good day and a better night for Claudia Brown, the best day and night of her life, and the incident of the talking crab drifted away into dream. There was no place for talking crabs in her world.

Miss Brown walked to Leo's party a little before nine on the evening of the fourteenth. She'd hesitated at the last minute, calling Vince, but he again insisted she go. A smiling Leo answered the door and guided her to the dining table, where he had placed a few mismatched pieces of dinnerware.

She seated herself. "So . . . where are the other guests?" she asked, as one might question a drop of rain on a cloudless day.

"Oh, it's just us," he said.

She attempted a smile, her upper lip ascending horse-like over her teeth. "I'm so glad you came to your senses, Leo. You'll be much happier in a home. They have puzzles and activities and sing-alongs. Doesn't that sound nice?"

"Sounds wonderful!" Leo nodded and looked at the clock on the mantle: 9:10. "I'll just go get the food," he said. "We're having crab for dinner." He walked through the kitchen, slipped out the door and locked it, then walked carefully and quietly around the house and locked the front door too. Earlier, he had closed all the curtains. As it was low tide, he went for a night walk on the beach.

Miss Brown thought it odd when she heard her host close the kitchen door. When he didn't return, she began to tap on her plate with a spoon. "Leo?" she called. "Leo?"

After a moment she heard little scratching and tapping sounds which soon swelled into a dozen, then a hundred, then it seemed a thousand scratching tapping sounds like rain on a pond. She sensed movement behind her and when she turned she saw them, thousands of the little creatures, covering the floor, the furniture, even the walls. "Crab for dinner," one of them said, and she could not deny that she heard it. Miss Claudia Brown screamed; and when she opened her mouth to scream again she gagged violently as something with many legs fell down her throat.

There was an investigation of course. The missing Miss Brown's client base was questioned, including Leo. She had walked the half-mile to his place from her house so her car was parked where it should be parked and Leo had taken his night walk to the Poseidon Lounge where Little Pete the bartender vouched for his presence. No evidence of foul play was ever found (crabs are very thorough), though a few eyebrows were raised when Leo's letter inviting the government worker to his party turned up among Claudia's things; but Leo claimed she never showed. Vince Gooden, who knew where Claudia was supposed to be on a certain night, said nothing, although it would now take him longer to acquire Leo's house. In the end he counted it a bit of luck that the woman was gone, for she'd begun to wear on him like a bad shoulder and he was glad to be rid of her.

Another worker was eventually appointed to replace Miss Brown, but she was an older woman awaiting retirement and, to Vince Gooden's irritation, did little aside from sit in the Poseidon lounge and have a drink or two, or several, every evening.

In the end, Leo kept his house and kept to himself (which was pretty much all he ever wanted). His friendship continued with the little crab and its descendants and friends (it saddened him to learn that fiddler crabs don't live very long). The crabs were grateful that he had provided such a feast, and, because of his kindness, he became a legend among them. For his part, Leo was happy for their company and had a great many enjoyable conversations with the little creatures, learning many things, unbothered by government workers.

Battle of Number Four

Ephraim Ponce with Bible

"Look around just before you cross onto the island. Men died there."
Ephraim Ponce – Private, CSA

The following two reports (original spellings) are from the actual war archives.

Partial Report of Major Edmund C. Weeks, Second Florida Cavalry (Union). Cedar Keys, Fla., February 16, 1865.

At 7 [o'clock] Monday morning, February 13, heard heavy firing at Station Four. Returned there as soon as possible; found our men flying in all directions; left an officer to halt and bring them up. Upon arriving at the trestle this side of Station Four I found some sixty of the Second Florida cavalry. I immediately pushed them across the bridge (the enemy were in possession of the end next to Station Four). At this time Captain Pease, with about forty men, all which remained with him, charged the enemy who were making an attack on our camp. The enemy, from 250 to 300 strong, with two pieces of artillery, commenced giving way. We took the bridge, and as soon as possible after crossing I deployed my men on the right and left of the road as skirmishers; drove the enemy gradually back until they broke and took to flight.

Partial Report of Capt. John J. Dickison, Second Florida Cavalry (CSA), Commanding South Florida Forces. Camp Baker, February 18, 1865.

The engagement soon became general, and lasted for about three hours and a half, during which time the enemy was defeated at all points; and the entire force, numbering about 600 in all, would have been slaughtered or captured but for the fact that ammunition for my artillery and some small-arms was entirely exhausted. The enemy occupied a position decidedly superior to that of ours, and although there was a disparity of numbers, in the ratio of five to one, the valor and intrepidity and superior prowess of my command caused the enemy to be defeated. Immediately after I fell back, induced, as I have stated above, by the lack of ammunition, and likewise on account of the fact that heavy re-enforcements had reached the enemy from Cedar Keys, he left the field of battle recipitately, leaving a portion of the dead and much plunder upon the field.

If you bother to read official reports and dispatches from officers, you will quickly smell a bunch of horse apples, scraped off boots and wiped on paper for higher-ups to sniff and nod over; self-congratulatory crap about how wonderful everything was during the battle, or engagement, or whatever they want to call it; how smart and brave everyone was, no matter how many men got kilt or grievously wounded following stupid orders. Them that actually fights don't get to write the reports. In truth, men just try to kill each other and live another day, and that's all there is to it. No official report ever said: *We kicked their asses, but it was all extremely stupid* or *we got our asses kicked and it was all extremely stupid.*

So I wrote my own report. I was there:

Report of Ephraim Ponce, Private (CSA) Cedar Keys, March 25, 1884.

We chased them Yanks all the way to the four channel where the track runs into Cedar Key. Though we was wore out, they'd stole a bunch of livestock and slaves and burned a bunch of stuff as they run from Levyville and we was anxious to discourage their cause, which I believe we surely did.

It was a clear morning with the rising sun behind us when we caught some of their force stuck on our side of the bridge. Captain Dickison gave the order and we commenced to firing, though they tried to hide behind the railroad embankment, which we pounded with our lone cannon. They knew they was in a fix, stuck as they was on our side of the trestle, and the remainder of their force tried to reinforce them, making for easy targets on the bridge. I seen that some of their soldiers was Negroes, which I had not encountered before. They seemed to fight just the same as everyone else. Far as I could tell, everyone's blood was red.

Finally, after about three hours, the Yanks'd had enough and was able to beat across the tracks back to the island. We might have followed except we would have exposed our own selves, and besides, we was almost out of shot.

I snuck forward some by myself to see what I might find and was surprised to hear a groan. It seems I'd come across an enemy straggler who was hiding in a palm thicket. I guess he was layin' low 'cause the man jumped up with a rattlesnake big as your thigh stuck on his neck. 'Course he yanked the monster away and you could see two streams of bright blood trickle from his neck. I raised my rifle and could've plugged him but I seen he was no threat and'd be dead soon enough.

I shot the snake instead. Who knows how many miles that Yank had travelled to get kilt by a snake? Life's funny.

The Yank, eyes big and moony, put his hand to his neck, then pulled it away and stared at it like he never seen his hand afore. Then he just fell down and began to thrash around as I reckon the poison seeped into his brain, or maybe his heart. Like I said, it was a big snake and the man'd got it in the neck. There was nothing I could do.

As he commenced to buck in the dirt, his hand shot out and grabbed my leg like he was trying to take me with him to the other side, and I admit I cursed him. Maybe I yelled a little 'cause I was scared. He grabbed my ankle so hard it seemed the Devil hisself had his claws in me and I lost my balance and fell onto my knees just like I was prayin'.

Then the snake-bit man looked into my eyes but I don't think he saw me, pulled my hand to his chest and made an awful sound, as if all the air in the world was leavin' his lungs. After a second, he arched his back and died. Amen.

I felt somethin' in his pocket where he'd pulled my hand and I opened his coat and took out a little gold locket. I opened it and saw a picture of a young woman and a few strands of hair bound with a thread resting on her picture. There wasn't no writin' on it anywheres.

As I turned the locket in my hand, I felt someone or something watching me and noticed a shade darker than the regular shades beneath the palmetto fronds where the soldier had burst forth. The dark shade was a woman and the woman was a Negress slave as sure as I'm a white fightin' man. She was lookin' at me with a face froze in fear and surprise. Lord knows what she'd been through.

I reckon she was one of the ones the Yanks had captured and had got left behind in the general melee of the fightin'. Now commenced the real Battle of Number 4. It was just me and her; my fellows, dog tired and out of shot, had retreated back into the mainland woods, and all the Yanks had run back over the trestle to lick their wounds.

It was one of them times. I just looked at her and she just looked at me like we was trying to figure it all out, which was impossible. Then she looked down to my rifle which I had not raised again – then back and forth from my face to weapon. It was one of those times I reckon, where decidin' is called for. Neither one of us moved or made a sound, just stared at each other like we was from different worlds. I guess we was.

To tell the truth, I'd never owned a slave and never wanted to. As I got older, I could see they was people right off, and ownin' someone just didn't seem like a right thing. Still, I enjoyed the things of slavery, the goods produced, the food grown, the labor of calloused hands. It gets complicated when you think about it too much.

I looked at the woman and I looked at the dead and snake-bit Yank at my feet, who already had little flies dancing on his glazed eyes, then I looked at the gold locket in my hands. The moment was comin' to an end.

"Here," I said, and tossed the locket to the woman who caught it easy, eyed it as she turned it over in her hand, then slid it down her brown bosom.

"You best lay low for a while," I said to the stolen property. "When it gets dark and quiet, you go over the trestle to the island. I reckon the Yanks will set you free or whatever it is they do with your kind."

She nodded and patted her chest where she'd dropped the locket. Then it was my turn to nod, and as I turned to go back to my world, the Negro slave woman stepped forward and took my hand. "E dupe," she said, which I took for "Thank you" in her kind of talk. She could have been calling me the son of a dog for all I knew, and I reckon I could not blame her.

"You're welcome," I said in my kind of talk.

Then she went back to her hidey place in the palmettos and I went to find my company and that was the real Battle of Number 4. We had driven the thievin' Yanks back and a human being had been set free by

Johnny Reb. Men had died and men had been wounded and asses had been kicked on both sides and it was all stupid.

Who won? I guess you could ask the snake-bit Yank, but he ain't sayin'. Or you could ask the Negress if you can find her.

Who won?

You could ask me, but I just don't know.

GILLS

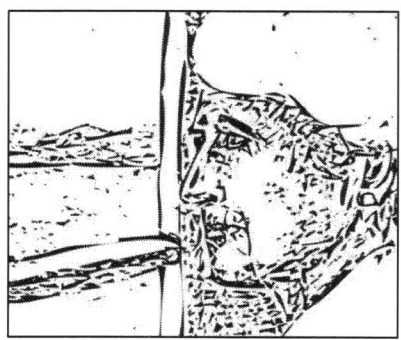

Sandy had gills. That's what she called the sagging skin at her jaw line and on her neck. Or maybe she had a wattle? Was it better to be a fish or a bird? She couldn't decide. She looked into the bathroom mirror, curled her lips into a smile, shook her head and watched the loose skin on her neck wobble from side to side.

"Okay," she said, "not a girl anymore." She hadn't been a girl for a long time. Decades. The wrapping was frayed, eyes crinkled, boobs and butt gone south. Disgusting word, she thought: gills. Just what every woman wants: gills. Probably even fish did not like gills, would prefer a plain old chin, a young neck. She reminded herself to look up the word and started to apply lipstick.

The kettle's whistle pierced the quiet and she went into the kitchen to make coffee. *This is a nice house that Edd's insurance purchased*, she thought. Outside the window, the Gulf of Mexico was pewter, doubling the gray clouds that drifted like puffy ships toward the mainland. A few lazy gulls sat on her decomposing dock, facing the breeze that was beginning to stir whitecaps.

Then she saw him and smiled. Bobby had returned, poling his skiff from boat to dock, the stern full of net and tubs of mullet sitting in the bottom. A dance, she thought, watching him move lightly from bow to stern, pushing the long pole along the side of the skiff, stepping on whatever surface was available. A misstep would send him into the water or break a leg. She could not understand how he kept the boat going straight when he pushed from the side.

At first it had surprised her, that she looked for him to come and go with the tide; it was not like her. (What *was* like her anymore?) She'd started to watch him almost as soon as she'd moved to the island, even checking the tide chart everyday so she could figure his comings and goings. She saw how the gulf light defined the muscles of his arms, like ropes that pulled and slackened as he poled the boat, his face hidden beneath a floppy straw hat and dark glasses. Miss Poteet, the widow fishwife, had told her how the fishermen tried to hide from the sun, fought it as much as the wind, its potency magnified by reflection from the water, coming at a man from two directions with cancer and cataracts. Curious, Sandy thought, the man had the same name as her son, though her son had insisted on being called Robert, even as a child.

Turning from the window, she pulled the heavy old dictionary from its shelf, laid it on the table and flipped through the dog-eared pages.

Gill: a respiratory organ found in many aquatic organisms that extracts dissolved oxygen from water, afterward excreting carbon dioxide. She touched the flesh beneath her chin.

In the bathroom she practiced jutting and lifting her head, trying to lessen the neck lines, but it only made her appear demented. She gave up and curled and fluffed her hair, then trimmed her bangs to more or less even. "Gills," she said, "the calling card of gravity."

She pulled on her dark slacks and a cream blouse, hesitated, then put on the pair of pearl earrings Edd had given her. She'd worn them every day since his passing, beginning with the funeral. Each time she put them on she said a prayer.

He was there, going to make a pot of coffee one Sunday morning just as he had every Sunday morning for years, and then he'd flopped down like a blanket thrown across the floor and he was not there anymore. Thirty-five years of marriage concluded by a blockage smaller than a pea.

It was Friday evening and she thought she'd walk down to the Poseidon Bar and listen to Guitar Joe play one of the two songs he knew, "Margaritaville" or "Sweet Home Alabama" (which he called Sweet Home Cedar Key). She laughed, thinking it funny that she was taking her gills to the Poseidon Bar. She must look him up, this god of the sea.

She rinsed her cup in the sink and looked toward Seahorse, the island across the bay. She could just see a spot of white, the old lighthouse. Out from the beach, Bobby's skiff was tied at his old boat house and he was gone.

There was a knock at the door. "Just a minute," she called touching a finger to her bangs. She opened the door to find Bobby standing with a wrapped newspaper package in his hand. Sandy opened her mouth, but nothing came out.

"Hello, Sandy," he said and waved the package at her. "I thought you might like some mullet." He held the fish out as if they were delicate things, some sort of offering. He had never come to her house before. She had never invited him -- had not been able to. She took the fish. "Why, thank you," she said, smiling and trying to look casual. Though he was on the stoop and she was in the doorway she could smell him, salt and sweat and fish and honest work, and she remembered how her father had smelled when she ran into his arms after he came home from work at the factory. She thought of Poseidon.

His brown eyes flickered and looked away. "You look nice," he said, as if he were remarking on the weather or the color of the sky.

She felt herself blush – didn't he see she was fat and old – that she had gills? "Thank you," she said. *Talk to him.* "I saw you come in and wondered –" He smiled and looked at her. "I wondered if you'd had any luck?"

"A little," he said. "You never really know, with luck or fish. You can't count on either one."

She wanted to say something profound, and then she remembered she'd only put lipstick on her top lip.

How surprised he'd be if he knew she looked for his boat, that she looked for him to go out or come in every day, that she knew exactly where and when he sat two pews behind her in the little Baptist church she'd started attending. Did he know that she suspected he might be staring at her in church? At first this alarmed her (they were, after all, in church). But the thought of him sitting behind her and watching her had given her an anticipation and pleasure she hadn't known for years, and, as usual, with the pleasure came guilt. Of course, she didn't really know if he was watching her; he was behind her, after all. Maybe it was just an old woman's imagination, but it was pleasurable and she enjoyed it, and it delighted her that she could enjoy anything again. Still, everything always mixed with the memory of Edd.

"Sandy?" It was Bobby's voice. "You okay?"

She nodded. "Getting old, I guess." She looked at the wrapped fish in her hand. An outboard motor gargled somewhere out on the gulf. *Don't tell him you're old, stupid! He can see you're old!*

Bobby smiled. There was a little pause, one of those times filled with possibility or with nothing. "Well, I guess I'd better get the catch to the fish house." He pointed to his gift. "Those will fry up real well. I've already cleaned 'em for you. I guess I'll see you in church." Then he nodded and walked toward the beach. *Ask him*, she scolded herself. *Ask him to come for dinner, then maybe a walk around the Big Dock. Maybe a sit and chat in the bar. That's why he brought the fish, you big dummy. You've already got yourself dressed.* But she said nothing, only stood silent as a channel marker and watched him disappear down the beach.

In the kitchen she unwrapped the fish and found four pearly fillets. Edd had enjoyed fishing, but she was unfamiliar with the saltwater kind, which seemed to overpower their freshwater kin, as the ocean overpowered the lake - deep, mysterious, dangerous – who really knew all that the ocean held? Like Cedar Key, she thought, salt air and mud eased into your pores, ready or not. It surprised her when tears came. She held them back until her eyes glistened.

That evening, Sandy sat in the Poseidon Bar sipping sherry. She wasn't really a drinker but had found she liked the sweetness of wine braced with brandy. Actually, that was a lie she liked to tell herself. She used to drink a great deal until she met Edd and settled into big-girl life. She sat at the bar because she felt sitting at a table underscored that she wanted company. The bar proper was made for the single person and that's what she was.

The bar occupied half the ground floor of the Sandbar Hotel, a building from the 1840s that had served as everything from a store to soldiers' quarters to a house of ill repute, or so it was said. The building had gone through a succession of owners, each adding or detracting as they thought best until it had evolved into a hotel. The other half of the first floor was a lobby, restaurant and kitchen. The rooms were upstairs and looked untouched from an earlier and simpler time.

Sandy studied the painting behind the bar, of Poseidon goofing off with two mermaids. The mermaids appeared delighted to be in the god's presence and she couldn't help but notice that Poseidon did look a little like Bobby, or Bobby looked a little like old Poseidon . . . minus the beard and long hair.

Of course, the mermaids were topless, half human and half fish, and Sandy wondered how they peed, how they bred, and why she was thinking logically about mythological creatures. But she knew mermaids existed because she'd seen one - the one and only time she and Edd had come to Cedar Key all those years ago – out in the channel while they dined at one of the dockside restaurants.

"Another drink?" asked Little Pete. He stood on skids behind the bar and looked up at her.

She shook her head. One was enough, though she knew she was only fooling herself. "Have you ever seen a mermaid, Pete?"

"I seen sea cows. Never a mermaid."

She laughed. She was becoming a sea cow. "I mean, do you think they exist?" The sherry warmed her like a hug.

"'There are more things in heaven and earth,'" he answered with a grin. Little Pete liked to quote things.

"What . . .?"

"'There are more things in heaven and earth, Horatio, than are dreamt of in your philosophy.' Hamlet said that to his friend after they saw his father's ghost. So yeah, I guess there could be mermaids. You seeing mermaids, Sandy?" He looked up at her and scratched behind his ear.

"Yep," she answered truthfully, the first time she'd told anyone besides Edd. She resumed studying the painting behind the bar and thought she saw Poseidon wink.

"You're doing what?" Robert had asked as they sat in her tiny kitchen in Pennsylvania.

"Moving to Florida. To a little island called Cedar Key."

"Where Hemingway lived?" Her son frowned and took a sip of coffee.

What lovely eyes, she thought, *his father's eyes*. "No. That's Key West. Cedar Key is a small island in the Gulf where there are no stop lights and very few stop signs. Travis McGee – that sort of thing."

"Travis who?"

"Never mind – I forgot how young you were."

"You know Key West is full of crime, Mom."

He was being obtuse. "No, dear – Cedar Key. Your Dad and I stayed there once after a business trip to Orlando." She didn't tell him what she had seen there. She'd never told anyone except Edd, and now Little Pete. But Edd hadn't laughed and that surprised her. She'd kept the memory tucked away, like a photo in the back of a drawer, comforted to know it was there, that she could take it out anytime she wanted.

She could not explain to Robert how the thought of moving, even though it frightened her, had begun to grow on her, a dream that solidified a little each day, a dream of someplace new and clean of memories (well, not all memories) -- where every object, every wall and corner did not remind her of the life she no longer possessed. She really couldn't even explain it to herself.

Robert wrinkled his nose as though he'd caught a bad smell, then rose and took his cup to the sink and rinsed it. "What's there?" he asked.

Something calling me. "Not much of anything as far as I remember," she answered. "Mostly water and slow, I believe."

"Slow is not a noun, Mom."

"It should be." She knew where the conversation was going, about leaving friends and family and all that was familiar, and at her age . . . but that was not a concern. She could always visit, could always return to the safety of the familiar. She wasn't going to another country, was she? She took her own cup to the sink and stood next to her son. "You can rent out the condo or sell it," she explained, waving her hand around the room like a real estate agent. "Indoor toilet. Hot water. Electricity."

He fake laughed. "Very funny."

She looked up at him over her glasses. "I'm quite serious, young man. It's time for a fresh start. And I'm tired of snow. That's why old folks move to Florida, you know."

He considered this for a moment. "I'll go with you," he offered.

"No. You have a firm, a very good firm. A *firm* firm." It was an old joke they shared.

"I'll take leave and – "

"You can help me move and even stay awhile, but you can't live there. We pushed you out of the nest and now I'm leaving the nest too. And isn't the law firm starting to land some big fish, my efficient and reliable son?"

"I'll take the bar in Florida – represent trophy wives in inheritance squabbles."

She opened the dishwasher and began to place silverware in its drawer, the stainless clinking as she dropped it in its slots. "Spoons. Forks. Knives." Order was soothing.

"Mom!"

"Everything in its place. Marry a jolly fat woman and come visit with a child under each arm. When I've had enough togetherness, crying and baby poop, I'll send you back up here and miss you terribly." She kissed his cheek then began to rinse the cups and put them away.

He looked at her, studied her as if he were deciding whether to take her case, or if he should ask the court to declare her insane. "I'm sorry," he said softly and there was a little pause and a little sigh as though the last bit of air had escaped his body. "I'm sorry Dad died."

Sandy stopped what she was doing and looked at her lawyer son. She nodded. "Somehow," she said, "it all goes on. I didn't believe that at first." She finished putting the creamer away. "But I don't think I'm done yet, Robert. My marriage is over but I'm not over – not yet. I'm still here. I'm still me . . . whatever that means. I just need to do something . . . different. Make a break."

Robert nodded and they hugged and she saw how he tried to hide his eyes from her; and then he'd gone off to his apartment in Concord because he had a big case the next day and a life of his own. She went to her room and started to pack.

After the sherry, Sandy walked home from the bar, undressed carefully, changed into her old shorts and t-shirt, and sat on her porch to watch the evening sky. The sun was setting behind Piney Point and splashed the underbelly of the clouds so that the world burned red. As the water darkened and the sky cooled to purple, she saw - or thought she saw - a figure out on the sand spit. The wind had brought the tide, and the figure seemed to be standing in shallow water. This was the way it happened before. . . a figure out in the water. Her chest tightened. She looked away, then back again. "Edd . . .?" She squinted, but the figure seemed to have long hair and couldn't be Edd; then, because the light had failed, had faded to make things formless and flowing, she saw nothing, only the imaginings of a lonely woman. Still, it gave her a sort of comfort, as though she were being tucked in for the night or pulling on a coat on a chilly morning. This surprised her.

The first time she'd seen it after her return to the island (after the business of the funeral and the move and the settling into the new house) had been as she sat on the Big Dock one evening. She had noticed a school of fish feeding and splashing out in the channel, only there was a human form too; and, like all those years ago when she'd visited with Edd, it was looking at her. Thinking someone might be in trouble, she'd run to the end of the pier and had seen nothing, only wave shadows or seaweed. After that, she habitually searched the chop of waves or the sawgrass along the shore, peering into the wake of a porpoise, staring at a crab trap float, just to make sure something wasn't looking back at her, that all was as it should be.

Sandy began Sunday morning dressing for church, which, as it was neither Christmas nor Easter, was not a dress-up occasion on the island; yet she wanted to look neither casual nor formal. *Like getting ready for a date*, she thought. It had been a long time since she'd actually dressed with a man in mind and she wasn't sure how to go about it. In the end, she chose black slacks and a loose white blouse because it hid her belly. She chose a shade of lipstick one shade brighter than she usually wore and made sure to apply it to both lips. *What do you think?* She asked the mirror. *What would Edd think?* He would say she was painting the old barn – Ha-ha! She put on her pearl earrings.

It was an early fall morning with the sun still low enough to cast soft shadows as she walked, and her boldness grew as she went down the little hill to the white board church. The business part of town sat beyond, Sunday sleepy and patient in the autumn air. She wondered if they used the word autumn in the south. A mockingbird alighted in a palm across from the church and began to practice.

According to habit, she arrived early and took her accustomed seat in the third row. There were only a few worshippers this early and Pastor Helms was gliding from one to the other, shaking hands and making obligatory small talk.

He made his way down an empty pew and stopped before her. "How are you, Miss Sandy?" he asked, smiling his sideways smile, as though something were pushing against his jaw. "Made up your mind yet about the teaching position?"

A few weeks ago, the pastor had approached her about the need for Sunday School teachers, and she'd begged off by telling him that she was still moving in and needed to get settled. She'd felt guilty (which is what Edd said church was for). Today, she smiled up at him and said, "Perhaps during the winter months." And he nodded and shook her hand and walked away to greet someone else. She really did mean to volunteer, though she wasn't sure teaching Sunday School was her forté. Perhaps she could help organize a bake sale or a clean-up project. She knew nothing about children anymore.

Then she turned around and there was Bobby, as she'd hoped, sitting where he always sat, two rows behind her and to the side, scrubbed and handsome. And there beside him sat a woman – a fly in her ointment. This was not part of the plan. If someone had been near Sandy, they would have heard her inhale sharply, as one does in one's sleep. She turned around quickly, took the hymnal from the rack in front of her and studied it intently.

She'd recognized at once that the woman was sitting *with* Bobby because she sat with the proprietary air women naturally recognize, a familiarity meant to show possession. For three months, Bobby Smeltzer had sat by himself, and on the one Sunday she'd made up her mind to invite him to do something he was sitting with a woman like they were... like a couple. The verb form of the word flashed through her mind and she felt guilty for thinking such thoughts in church.

The introductory hymn began, tinkling notes scattering over the congregants like rain. Pastor Helms sang loudly in an effort to warm up the service. No one would know that Sandy was a mess: she stood and sat as directed and appeared to participate, even moving her lips during the singing, but no sound came forth. She heard none of Pastor Helms' sermon — something about Potiphar's wife -- hearing instead an internal dialogue that accused her of being an old fool. An angry fool, she thought, almost dropping the offering plate. Why didn't I pay attention to him sooner, show him a little attention? She laid her bulletin on the pew and pretended to brush something off her shoulder, glancing back to see the woman, who was looking back at her. The woman smiled and nodded - with, Sandy thought, a shade of challenge behind her overly painted blue eyes. Bobby looked straight ahead and appeared to be listening to the sermon. After the benediction, Sandy slipped out the side door and walked briskly home.

The tide receded that evening. The sky was marbled with darkening pink clouds, and a small flock of birds scavenged along the spit, running ahead and away from her as she walked, stepping over conch eggs (broken necklaces, she thought), pieces of shells and ubiquitous sand dollars, waves lapping as the water withdrew to follow the moon. She saw something far out on the spit, but as she stared it turned into ... what ... a piece of driftwood.

Her house felt cold and dark and she went to bed early.

The following afternoon she ran into *the* woman - the *other woman* - in the Zippy store. Bobby's new woman, as she'd come to think of her. There were only a few aisles, which made it impossible to hide, and it embarrassed Sandy that she should even think of avoiding the woman, as though she were a rival -- there was nothing between her and Bobby, and what the woman did was her business. Well, almost her business. What one did in Cedar Key was everyone's business; such is the way of island towns.

Sandy had hardly moved in when the flotsam of gossip began to wash her way. There were the usual widows (like Miss Poteet) who made everyone's business their business, and there was a Women's

Club that she didn't care to join (Sandy was convinced they existed only for the purpose of gossip). Miss Poteet kept her informed well enough. Still, she suspected there was something about an island, about being surrounded by the muddy gulf, that provoked chatter and speculation disguised as friendliness, sharp and barbed as a ray's sting.

"So nice to see you in church," she said to the woman when she found the meeting inevitable in the little store. It comforted her to see that without makeup the woman appeared plain, even a little tired. A few miles on her, Edd would have said. Just so, the woman did not appear to have even the beginning of gills.

"Yes. Bobby's been after me to go forever and I just kept putting him off." The woman smiled. "I'm Mary Ellen," she said, extending her hand. "Tell you, after working all week I'm just worn out by Sunday morning. You wouldn't think art would wear on you, but it does. Saturdays have just been crazy." Miss Poteet had mentioned that a woman, an artist, had moved out to Hudson Hill recently. She'd said something about the woman making free-form sculptures out of driftwood, which Sandy thought was silly because driftwood was already sculpted by wind and wave.

"I'm Sandy Collins," Sandy said, taking the woman's hand, feeling for a ring. There was a brief pause and both women smiled as women do and then, "Well, I'll see you later, Mary Ellen." Then she went to study the lunchmeat in the refrigerated section.

That evening, Sandy called Robert. She liked to picture their voices bouncing along the miles of telephone line between Cedar Key and Concord, little atoms flying back and forth like BBs in a hose.

"Hello, Son – and yes – everything is fine." She never called him on Mondays and didn't want him to think something was wrong. Of course, nothing was wrong.

"Hey. Just walked in." She heard a female voice in the background, then his voice away from the receiver.

"I can call later, Robert, if this -"

"No--No--Cheryl was talking to me from the kitchen and didn't know I was on the phone."

"Cheryl?"

"No, you haven't met her, Mom. She works in the Public Defender's office and we are going to fix whatever we can find for dinner."

This is what she got for moving away. She wanted to talk, to be a part of his life, but it was too late. She was not there, and he was living his life. What did she expect him to do?

"You okay?" he asked. She heard music in the background. The Doors played "Light My Fire," though she didn't know that was the name of the song.

"I said I'm fine, dear. Just wanted to say 'Hello.' Listen – you've got company. Why don't I call you this weekend and we'll chat then?"

"You're sure you're all right?"

"Just fine, Son. Give my love to . . ."

"Cheryl."

"Cheryl. And remember: a fat one with a baby under each arm."

"Funny. Goodnight, Mom."

"Goodnight, Robert. Love you." Hanging up the phone can be a sad thing, she thought.

Sandy busied herself during the week, cleaning and washing things that were clean and washed, trying to forget that she was upset over something that didn't even exist, that she was behaving like a silly teenager. A dormant part of her had awakened and she had no idea how to deal with it. She went for long walks, out to the airport and to the ancient cemetery to wander among the clamshell-covered graves. She went to the little state museum, but she did not walk past the woman artist's house on Hudson Hill. She walked around the big dock and watched the gulls scavenge tidbits from the fishermen and tourists. She spoke to no one (as Miss Poteet had gone to visit her sister in Atlanta), only exchanging polite pleasantries when she bought her groceries or slipped her mail out of the box at the post office. She still watched for Bobby, but the weather had been rough for a week and she only saw him go out a few times. Robert had begun to call frequently, and she knew he was worried about her because it was the topic of every conversation, though she did her best to act cheerful and project a carefree attitude whenever he called. He insisted she come visit him or he was going to come down and visit her. She protested that she was fine and was still adjusting to island life, which was true, she thought. She began to attend church less and less.

In any case, busyness could only take her so far and that's when it happened, when one chilly Friday night she found herself in the Poseidon lounge listening to Guitar Joe sing about Margaritaville for the fifth time and she ordered a second sherry, which to most meant absolutely nothing, but to Sandy it was a crossing of the border, a finger pulled from the dyke, a spin of the cylinder, as significant as a dieter having a second slice of pie or a smoker deciding to smoke just one after a decade of abstinence – she knew, though she would not admit, the second sherry would send her on her way.

As she sipped, she focused on the painting behind the bar. Poseidon had his arm around the redheaded mermaid while the blonde mermaid poured him a drink. Sandy thought she might dye her hair red. It seemed grossly unfair to her that Poseidon had legs, while the mermaids had to make do with scales and a flapping tail. *What could ol' Poseidon do with them*, she thought, *they don't have the necessary parts!* A rosy glow seemed to emanate from the painting, filling her with warmth and sadness. She ordered another sherry.

After a while, when the clock had spun toward closing, she walked a little unsteadily to Guitar Joe and asked him if he knew the song Louie, Louie. She asked because she knew from her youth that the song only had three chords. He said he didn't but would try to learn it as he didn't get many requests.

"Ceee . . . Efffff . . . and Geeee," she said, mouthing each word slowly as if Joe were deaf and it might help him remember the progression. Then she turned, snapped a salute to Little Pete who was mopping behind the bar, and went out the door. She did not see him look at the painting behind the bar and nod his head.

She decided to walk along the beach on the way home rather than taking the road up 2nd Street. Although it was chilly, she leaned against a beached skiff and pulled her shoes off, enjoying the coolness of the sand as it molded to her feet. She saw that the tide was low, but the offshore breeze was quickening, and she knew from her tide chart that it would soon turn. She walked toward the spit, fiddler crabs making way, the males waving their one huge claw. In the moonlight, lines of seaweed from the last high tide ran before her as if to guide her down the beach. The breeze smelled like sad and long-ago music, and she pulled her windbreaker tight. Though it was dark except for the moon, she made out a few shapes (dolphins?) gamboling in the channel and envied them, their uncluttered lives and their freedom.

She looked over the water, and knew it was there and waiting for her, out off the spit. She left the beach and walked over the mud, leaning into the wind now, and did not notice fingers of lightning probing the clouds behind Piney Point. There! She saw it! Something in the water out as far as you could go, at the very end of the spit. *Stay there*, she willed the figure. *I'm coming to you. Just a little closer.* Then the squall came over the point and brought stinging darts of rain that made tiny clapping sounds in the waves. She walked in water, not caring that the tide was changing and, quickened by the wind now, would rush in to blanket the spit for the night. Between the crescent of the moon and the lightning flashes, she thought she could just make out…she stumbled over something in the water, a clump of shell, a piece of wood, and a sharp pain stabbed through her foot. She fell forward, throwing her hands out, going under in the rising water, waves flooding her eyes with salt, burying her.

Though the water was dark and cold and the unknown moved around her, she felt at peace; and though it may have been the sherry, it came to her how silly she'd been, concocting fantasies in place of acceptance and reality. Oh, how she'd missed the warmth of alcohol, the sense of certainty that comes with the soothing liquid, false though it might be. Something Little Pete had said came to her at the very moment she was . . . was what? Drowning? She thought she might still stand; surely the angry water was, maybe, only chest deep. *Besides*, she thought, *I have gills*. "That that is, is," Little Pete had told her. Shakespeare or something. She wanted to stay on the bottom and sit like a stone in the lap of the muddy gulf until she could sit no longer, and then . . . sit some more. She considered her circumstances, and though her lungs burned in her chest and the cold did its numbing work on her body, she decided that, yes, that is what she would do, she would sit and roll with the gelid tide until the very end. And then she would be with Edd where she belonged. She had been a fool to think she could start over. You could cover a scar with makeup, but it was still a scar.

Bolts from the squall (on top of her now) began to arc across the black sky like tridents. Something swam by in a flash of blue light, as though it had a light of its own, lit from within. She'd read that sharks fed at night and therefore one should not swim then, much less sit on the briny bottom. *Mustn't sit on your briny bottom!* She closed her burning eyes and when she opened them she was staring into the lightning-lit face of a ... of a female ... of a woman, long hair waving in the water, breasts no bigger than oranges. She felt a sharp tug and pain shot through her ears, then something – hands? -- pushed her. She kicked out and could not find the bottom and felt herself being lifted toward the rising and falling light. Her face broke the water and she gulped a huge breath before a wave slapped her hard, forcing black water up her nose ... and the world narrowed down to a simple, airless nothing.

Shivering. Cold. Teeth clicking. Her left foot was on fire. From somewhere came the throb of a diesel engine. A blanket around her. A man held a light and peered into her face. Bobby. He was soaked. Had he been on the spit too?

"You picked a heck of a time for a swim, Sandy. Most folks don't swim in the channel at night during a squall."

"Bobby?"

"I was trying to beat the storm in and heard – saw, really – a lot of commotion – figured it was porpoise feeding. Shone my light and there you were, bobbing like a crab trap buoy – covered in seaweed. What in the world –- you looked like a mermaid."

"We're almost in," called a female voice. "How's she doing?"

He shone the flashlight into her face again. "She'll live, Mary Ellen."

"Mary Ellen ... "

"You know my cousin, Mary Ellen. She said you met in the Zippy store. Sometimes she goes out with me – steers us in while I clean the boat. Keeps her off the streets." A pretend laugh came from the cabin. "This squall snuck up on us."

Sandy grimaced and tried to sit up and touch her bleeding foot. His *cousin?*

"You lost some skin there," Bobby said, straightening her leg. "Looks like you decided to kick some barnacles or oysters or something."

Then, warmed by the blanket and the mumbled voices of Bobby and Mary Ellen and the throb of the diesel, Sandy closed her eyes and thought she dreamt as the boat rocked and made its way through the storm to the island. Finally, the engine died, and she felt herself lifted onto a bouncing skiff which Bobby poled straight onto the beach. Then he carried her to her house as Mary Ellen followed in the swirling rain.

As Bobby laid her in her bed, she wondered if he could smell the alcohol on her breath, but if he did, he said nothing. Mary Ellen went to make tea. Bobby picked some seaweed out of her hair and when he pulled her hair back his eyes widened. He touched her ear lobes and said, "You are a woman of mystery, Sandy Collins." He held up his index fingers and she saw that they were spotted with blood.

"My pearls!" she cried.

She felt her earlobes and found them empty, bleeding where the posts had been ripped from the flesh. Yet her ears did not hurt.

Bobby looked at her closely. "The Gulf took your pearls," he said. "We'll get you some more." They paused as they looked at each other and listened to the rain tattooing the tin roof. He laid his hand over hers.

"No," she said softly. "No more pearls." She thought she heard a splash somewhere far away, as though something large had entered the water and disappeared. Bobby frowned and shook his head as though he heard it too. "Gone forever," she whispered.

"You sure you're okay? I could run you to the hospital in Gainesville."

She breathed deeply and liked the way Bobby's hand felt over hers. Strong. Tender. She was, she knew, just fine. No, she wasn't just fine, not yet, but she knew she would be. She placed her other hand over Bobby's and smiled and he quickly looked away. Mary Ellen entered with the steaming tea.

Outside, the tide began to turn.

CATBIRTH

No one actually saw Margaret give birth to a kitten. If you asked, they would say that everyone knows women cannot do such things. Still, if some dared tell you what they believed, it would be quite different. Sometimes such things happen out of great love, out of the heart.

In any case, and whatever you choose to believe, Margaret gave birth to a kitten. She sat up one morning in her single bed and there it was. There was very little blood.

After her surprise (and some wonder), she wrapped the kitten in a towel, sat it near a window for warmth, pulled the dropper from an old bottle of medicine, rinsed it, and filled it with milk and a little sugar. At first the kitten resisted but when it tasted the sweet liquid it began to suckle.

In a week the kitten opened its eyes and Margaret saw they looked like green ice, as though they'd been frozen and dropped into hot water. At first she thought the kitten was blind but was relieved when she saw the creature following her around the room, first with its grass-colored eyes and then with small and hesitant steps. *It thinks I am its mother*, she thought. Then she remembered that she *was* its mother and no longer felt lonely.

She filled a shirt box with sand so the kitten would have a place to go to the bathroom and then crumpled newspaper into a ball so it would have something to bat around. It took a while for it to do these things. Eventually, after a month or so, the cat ate what Margaret ate, though she was careful to cut its food into small bits. If it was a tough meat, she chewed it first before placing it in front of the little kitty. It didn't seem to mind.

The cat grew, of course, and at first just sat on her lap, then discovered pleasure in riding on her shoulder and finally, on its own accord, climbed atop her head and nested in her unkempt brown curls, clinging onto hair but not flesh. This was how it started -- the beginning -- though it is difficult to separate the beginning of a thing from what preceded or followed. Edges are only illusions.

Margaret claimed odd jobs: she cleaned houses, pulled weeds, cleaned the Poseidon bar, cooked fish and grits at restaurants, and began doing her work with the cat on her head. She even began to walk around the dock or to the Zippy store with the cat perched over her brow. (She taught it to keep its tail to the side or back of her head so she could see.) She even drove her old car with the cat on her head (though she had to lean to the right to give the cat room). At first, she drew stares and laughs but after a while most paid no mind, such is the power of familiarity. Once, on a dare, Mean Freddie sneaked up behind Margaret, intending to knock the cat from her head, but the cat turned to face the boy and something in its frozen stare stayed Freddie's hand in mid-swing. He sheepishly looked back to the boys watching him, shook his head and ran home.

It is certain that Margaret enjoyed the cat, and as she never did anything to her hair it made no difference in her grooming. She saw the cat as a sort of living hood ornament, like the ones that graced old cars: instead of an eagle or an Indian chief on her hood, she had a cat upon her head and she wore it proudly.

One day a reporter from the Gainesville paper arrived to write a story and take photos of Margaret with the cat on her head. She posed before the old hotel and at the little post office and down by the sand spit. The story went statewide and even ran nationally for a few days, but Margaret never read or watched the news and did not care that there was interest in the cat on her head. To Margaret, the cat sitting on her head was no different than breathing or walking.

"I gave birth to you," she told the cat. "How did that happen?" The cat jumped from her head and lay at her feet, purring.

Of course, others on the island began wearing cats on their heads – or trying to. As they had not given birth to the cats, the animals would not stay in place -- they were, after all, cats -- so someone began knitting cat caps and soon many women and some men were wearing these on their heads. A writer for a northern travel magazine arrived to do a story on Margaret and the island's cat-on-head phenomenon and when it was published the Margaret Cat-On-The-Head Movement was born. A man in Palatka began hand-raising and training kittens to sit on heads and the movement spread. Protesters were seen on the news shouting angrily for or against this or that with cats or cat facsimiles on their heads. Newborns wore cat caps for their first hospital pictures. Smiling brides wore cat tiaras.

Agents found Cedar Key and approached Margaret for trademark and copyright and merchandising and all manner of rights, but Margaret did not understand them, cared for none of it, and stopped answering her door. Lawyers called, offering to represent her, and a ghost writer asked to turn her story into a novel. After she called Pastor Helms and asked if he would arrange to have her mail and groceries delivered once a week, she unplugged her phone. The joy the cat had brought into her life began to dissipate like air from an old tire. She was seen less around town and then only in the evening or at night. Though life would certainly be easier, it troubled Margaret when she thought of going without the cat. *No*, she thought, *I am its mother. It is my cat. Why must I change? I only want to wear the cat on my head. Is that such a terrible thing?*

The mayor and the town council decided to hold a Cat-On-The-Head festival. Artists were invited: there would be Cat-On-The-Head paintings, Cat-On-The-Head sculptures, and cat-shaped caps. The Women's Club could sell "world famous" CATfish sandwiches. Every room on the island was booked. Artificial-looking TV reporters walked around town trailing cameramen. Maps were sold to Margaret's house and a bus tour passed by every half hour, packed with visitors hoping to glimpse the lady with the cat on her head. All they saw was a closed house with drawn drapes. Reporters and tourists knocked on her door but there was no answer.

"But Margaret," Pastor Helms explained, "the town is proud. You've put us on the map."

Margaret stopped rocking and stared at him from beneath the cat, its paw swishing across her face like a windshield wiper. This didn't seem to bother her. "Weren't we already on the map?" she asked.

"A figure of speech, Margaret. Folks are having fun. You should see all the cat stuff they're making and selling. We . . . *you* are big news!"

"I don't want to be big news. I just want to have the cat on my head. Is that a crime?"

The pastor sighed. "No — of course not. It's just that the town cannot very well have a Cat-On-The-Head festival without the Cat-On-The-Head Lady . . . and that's you, Margaret." Pastor Helms raised an eyebrow. "You still say you gave birth to the cat?"

"Yep."

"Metaphorically, of course."

"I don't know about that, but I gave birth to the cat — 'course it was smaller then -- a kitten."

"I see. . . Well, all they want you to do is make an appearance at the park on Sunday, the final day of the festival. There will be a bonfire and music, fireworks and food. You won't have to do anything. Just stand on the podium with the cat on your head and let the mayor babble for a minute and present you with a certificate or something. That's it."

He watched her close her eyes and shake her head. He did not really blame her. She just wanted to walk around with a cat on her head; there was no harm, and poor Margaret was just being herself, a bit mad perhaps . . . but aren't we all in one way or another? He had an idea.

"Look," he said. "Let's get you in one of the condos across from the park. My brother rented one for the festival and I'm sure he wouldn't mind. Third floor - You could watch the proceedings and then perhaps step out on the balcony and wave --"

"With the cat on my head," she interrupted.

"Of course. That's the point! And no one, except me - and my brother, of course - will know where you are. I'll tip off the mayor at the last moment and he can announce your appearance on the balcony. You can step out, give a little wave, then go away. The crowd will be satisfied. What do you think?"

She stared at him a moment, thinking. "No speaking?" she asked.

"Not a word if you don't want to."

"If I do this . . .will they let me alone?"

Of course not, the pastor thought. *They will never leave you alone. You go around with a cat on your head!* But he was a kind man and didn't say this. He had learned, as a shepherd of souls, that it is often better not to speak.

Margaret resumed her rocking. "Alright," was all she said.

The Cat-On-The-Head festival was a great success. Things were bought and sold, acquaintances were made and plans were laid for a bigger and better festival the following year. As Margaret had kept herself unseen since the announcement of the festival, visitor interest was heightened when it was announced she would appear, and the locals who actually knew her held court, posing for photographers and news crews as they proudly related exaggerated tales of their dear Margaret, who was now everyone's best friend.

On Sunday evening, the finalé at the park was ready: bunting was hung, cat hats were worn, Guitar Joe played the two songs he knew and the gathering hummed in anticipation of celebrity. Networks from Tampa, Orlando and Gainesville were on hand, and a dozen county and state officials were sprinkled about. When Pastor Helms went to pick up Margaret he found her house empty. A note was stuck on the door:

> *The cat has runned away. I have gonn to find it.*
> *You'r friend, Margaret*

"Uh-Oh," said the pastor as he left to look for the guest of honor.

When Pastor Helms finally gave up, he went to the park, where the festivities, aided by alcohol, were ratcheting toward the finalé. The Best Cat Hat (artificial cat) and Best Cat Hat (live cat) had been awarded. The Women's Club had fattened their treasury by selling feline funnel cakes and hair ball candies while henna artists painted cat paw prints on hundreds of cheeks. Pastor Helms stood on the bandstand with the mayor, who was frowning.

"What do you mean, 'She's gone'? She has to appear in five minutes, right up there on that balcony!" He motioned toward the condos across the street. "It's the finalé of the whole event – fireworks, balloons, everything."

The pastor shrugged. "The cat ran off. She went to look for it. I can't find her."

The mayor looked at Pastor Helms. "Are there any prayers for lost cats?" he asked. The mayor considered church a waste of time (except during the election season) and made no distinction between Protestant and Catholic.

Just then the high school band began a spirited medley of Stephen Foster tunes. The last song, "Suwanee River," would be the mayor's cue to speak and introduce Margaret.

"Saints are a little out of my league, Mayor. I mean there's Saint Francis – he did all the animals." The pastor paused. "And there's a Gertrude – I think she specialized in cats. I'm Protestant."

"Okay – try her," the mayor said. "My grandmother's name was Gertrude. Might work. Just find Margaret," he whispered through clenched teeth, smiling and waving at the crowd.

The band sounded its last discordant notes and the crowd looked to the podium.

A movement caught the pastor's eye and he turned to see his cousin waving from third floor condo. The cousin nodded his head up and down.

"She's here!" the pastor whispered.

"What?"

"Margaret is here. She made it." He pointed up to his cousin.

"Thank Gertrude!" said the mayor. Then he smiled and stepped to the microphone. The crowd quieted as he cleared his throat.

"Fellow Cedar Keyans," he began, "and visitors from afar. I welcome you to the first, but certainly not last, Cat-On-The-Head festival. I know – "

There was a gasp and several hands motioned toward the balcony. "There she is!" someone yelled. Margaret stood on the little balcony, staring, holding one arm behind her back, a dark smear on the front of her shirt.

"We haven't done the fireworks!" the mayor said to Pastor Helms. "She comes after the fireworks!"

"Just go with it," Helms whispered. The crowd edged across the street to the condos. The mayor, losing his audience, opened his mouth to continue but another shout from the crowd cut him short. Margaret held something before her, like a child showing a broken toy to a parent. Everything was silent, the waves that lapped the little beach, the parents, children, the drunks, the mayor, even the raucous gulls held their peace.

"I found my cat," Margaret shouted. "It had run across the road. It was coming home."

"What happened?" floated from the assembled.

Margaret began to swing the thing she held, her own awful pendulum. "When it saw me, it started to come home – to cross the street. Then a tour bus rounded the corner. The driver hit the brakes but it scared the cat. It run under the bus." Understanding formed, condensed on foreheads and hairlines. Some gasped with realization.

On the balcony Margaret began to swing the thing around her head in circular motion, then, after a minute, yelled and flung it across the road and into the park. As it landed it appeared to wiggle. Women screamed. The mayor threw up. Men gagged and shouted and a reporter tripped as she ran to where the thing landed. A ring of people formed. Cameramen elbowed to the spot but found only sandspurs and gravel. There was nothing there.

Faces turned to the balcony. They looked at Margaret and she looked back at them, then turned and left and went to her empty house, sat down in her chair and rocked. She never mentioned the cat again.

She had returned it to her heart, where it was born.

PICTURES OF JESUS

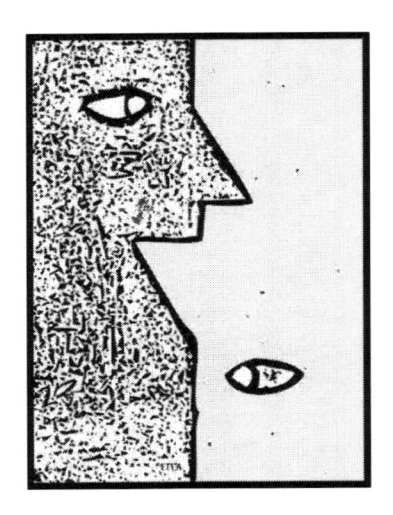

"RACIAL VIOLENCE ERUPTED IN THE SMALL AND QUIET ROSEWOOD COMMUNITY JANUARY 1-7, 1923."

"THOSE WHO SURVIVED WERE FOREVER SCARRED."

-- FROM ROSEWOOD FLORIDA HERITAGE LANDMARK SIGN

Pastor Helms arrived early at the Baptist Holiness Church to prepare communion, and as he placed the elements on the serving table he looked up and saw that the picture which hung on the wall by the piano had changed. Jesus was now black.

He walked to the picture, a copy that hung on walls in a thousand homes and churches — the knocking Savior standing at the door. He cautiously touched the face, testing for paint or the smell of some joker's black marker. Then he saw that the Jesus was not just colored black, but that he had African features: a real Black Jesus, not a Caucasian Jesus colored black.

The pastor grabbed the sides of the frame to lift the picture from the wall but it would not move. Puzzled, he stared at the image, then heard something behind him and turned to see the church pianist, Mrs. Nancy, open mouthed, dropped music leafing to the floor. Helms smiled and shrugged and wondered how he could incorporate this into his sermon, which was to begin in thirty minutes.

That evening, when the members of the tiny church in Otter Creek, the Sanctified Church of Africa, heard about the Black Jesus in Cedar Key, they had a mighty congregational laugh. "'Bout time," said Brother Samuels, imagining the look on the Baptists' faces. He had a double laugh when told that the picture would not come off the wall – although he had no idea how that could be.

"Amen," said Sister Harper. Sister Harper said "Amen" to everything, good or bad. She was Sister Amen.

No one laughed in the Sanctified Church of Africa the next Sunday when they arrived and saw that the church's painting of its Savior, dressed in colorful African garb and proclaiming the Good News on the banks of the Jordan was no longer a midnight Moor but had morphed into a white man -- Caucasian and pink as the bottom of their feet.

Various church members took turns trying to remove the picture, but it would not budge. No one heard Brother Samuels' sermon that morning, as eyes shifted from the preacher to the blue-eyed Jesus that watched them from the wall.

News travels both ways, of course, and the members of the Baptist Holiness Church were relieved and not a little amused themselves that the prankster, whoever he was, had achieved a sort of racial balance. Yet underneath the humor, both congregations were frightened: it unsettled them that someone could steal into their sanctuaries and . . . change things; and this change watched from the wall. The religious are wary of change.

Brother Samuels tried a pry bar on his church's picture, but the bar became unexplainably hot and he had to drop it. Pastor Helms' idea was to cut out the section of wall around the picture, but nothing would penetrate the drywall and he gave up, reluctant to damage God's house.

Both congregations began to whisper of miracles, and this frightened both leaders. Miracles were fine in the Bible, in historical context, but that was long ago and surely mostly symbolic. Neither church was of the faith that venerated objects. They were proudly Protestant and averse to hocus-pocus.

As the news spread, both churches began to draw the curious, those who'd never shadowed a church doorway or sat in a pew. At the Baptist Holiness Church, Mrs. Nancy suggested charging admission of one dollar on Sundays to anyone not of the congregation who wanted to view the black image.

In Otter Creek, Brother Samuels cautiously embraced his little church's unexpected fame. It encouraged interest in the Lord, but he knew the proclivity of folks to seek and sensationalize the novel, and perhaps (he was beginning to admit), the miraculous. He reasoned that was why the Lord hid the ark and the cross – folks would just worship those things and not the Spirit behind them.

Weeks passed. One rainy evening Brother Samuels and Sister Amen stood before the picture. "They chargin' money to look at the Baptist church," Brother Samuels said (though it had only been a suggestion on the part of Mrs. Nancy and not acted upon; such is the nature of untested rumor). "I don't think I want to do that."

"Amen," said the sister. "Wouldn't be right."

Brother Samuels considered this. "Well, it ain't wrong – I hear they usin' the money to buy paint for some of the members' houses. Salt air and wind takes its toll."

"Amen," said Sister, shifting her eyes to the collection of worn chairs behind the pulpit. "'Course, we could sure use some chairs for the choir."

Brother Samuels turned and started for his tiny office. "I got to make a phone call," he said.

"Amen," said Sister Amen.

Pastor Helms answered the knock on his study door and was surprised to see Brother Samuels standing on the stoop holding a gallon of white paint in each hand. Brother Samuels lifted the heavy cans a few inches and said, "Heard some of your folks could use paint? Heard about the fund raisin'. So, I thought we'd help out." There was a pause as both men looked at each other.

Pastor Helms finally said, "That's kind of you, Brother Samuels. Won't you come in? And let me help with that paint. How about some coffee? I'll ask Clarice to make some."

"That'd be fine," said Brother Samuels and set the cans inside the door.

"And then I'll show you the picture."

After coffee and the viewing, the two men sat in the sanctuary and talked.

The road to Otter Creek was straight and empty, and Brother Samuels drove slowly. The Black Jesus he'd just seen in the white house of worship was just as much a Black Jesus as the image in his own church was a White Jesus. He'd suspected trickery, and was relieved to learn that Pastor Helms was not charging admission to view the picture. Then he frowned; it was too coincidental that the figure would change in both churches. Again, he considered that it might be a miracle, but he pushed away the thought and slapped at the idea as one might slap at a mosquito. He knew there was little chance of white church members venerating a black man or of black church members bowing to a white man – even if that man was Jesus.

It took several phone calls and meetings for the two leaders to decide the congregations would come together in Rosewood. This was not a simple thing, and many phone calls and meetings followed in each church. Perhaps, the pastor and the brother suggested, they might find a way to remove the pictures, make an exchange, and all would be well. The meeting was held in front of the very house that figured in the infamous Rosewood Massacre. The site had not been casually chosen.

Tables and chairs were set out and a bonfire was built. The Otter Creek congregation assembled on one side of the fire and the Cedar Key congregation on the other.

Slowly, as though obeying some ancient ritual -- the southern sacrament of Sunday dinner -- women began to bring food from their vehicles: fried chicken, biscuits, potato salad, smoked fish, gallons of tea, turnip and mustard greens, pigs' ears and pigs' feet and all manner of cakes and sweets.

After Sister Amen blessed the food with a lengthy and emphatic prayer, the races began to meld around the laden tables, two currents forming a larger stream. Plates in hand, the congregations – hesitantly at first – sat with each other, speaking cautiously, politely, wondering at the history of the place. As the shadows grew, the bonfire was fed, licked upward, drove back the mosquitoes and lit every face. Pieces of conversation smoked the air. A guitar appeared, a mouth harp, a banjo, spoons. Music.

Someone began to sing in a high voice and others joined, the old hymn everyone knew, and the night grew until only the fire and faces remained, some darker, some lighter, all singing.

Sister Amen later said the flames took the shape of wings, thrusting skyward. Others felt a presence around and within them as the circle of people sang and faced the fire, something unseen yet palpable. When the last note floated away, Pastor Helms and Brother Samuels stood to address the assembled and found they could not speak, both dumb as Zechariah, silent as disbelief.

As the congregations stared, the two men opened and closed their mouths like fish, but made no sound. Finally, they looked at each other, shook hands, and nodded.

"Amen," said Sister Amen.

Both congregations went to their homes, full of questions and doubt and hope. The next morning, after a long night, the church leaders discovered that they could speak again and that their respective pictures had fallen, undamaged, to the floor.

Meetings were quickly called. By congregational vote both pictures were rehung: in the white church, Black Jesus stood at the door and knocked; in the black church, White Jesus addressed the jubilant and colorful assembly on the banks of the Jordan.

The two congregations began to meet together: Pastor Helms would lead a caravan to the Sanctified Church of Africa or Brother Samuels would lead a caravan to the Baptist Holiness Church. After short sermons (this in itself was miraculous), all would visit and look at the other church's picture of Jesus, at the Savior who looked like them.

TWO HEARTS

They were silent on the drive to the coast from Gainesville and they were silent now, standing on the beach at the little park and packing only the necessary into kayaks for the overnight trip. He'd told her they needed to be together – just the two of them. Things change on an island, he'd said.

Finished packing, they pushed off, stepping carefully into their little vessels, paddling as only the young can, without ache or pain, carving "V"s in the water; he, bent forward, earnest, shoving the water behind him; she, as a bird, simple, effortless. The gulf was flat and grey and reflected nothing.

The man was glad to escape the shore and the biting things. A mullet flashed out of the water in front of them and, off to the west, a porpoise gamboled and splashed. They paddled silently, stopping only to drink and rest tired muscles.

In the evening they landed on the little island at high tide. Tide was everything. Low water meant pulling and wrestling loaded kayaks through deep mud. Always, the biters returned with the land, called to feast by flesh.

"Where's the bug stuff?" he asked, his voice out of place and loud. He slapped a mosquito on his arm, smearing blood.

"In your kit," she said. She missed her phone. He'd told her that phones intrude.

She pointed to higher ground. "There's a flat place – for the tent." Once, when they were novices, they'd pitched the tent on a little hill and had rolled to the lower side all night; they'd laughed and laughed, and it had been great fun.

"You want some?" he said, waving the repellent.

"They're not bothering me."

They pulled things from the kayaks – ground cover, tent, sleeping bags, a gas stove, cans of food, and put it all together properly so they could spend the night. As they worked, the sun fell and the strip of mainland faded to grey, though the sun side of the gulf dusted yellow.

"You can get the stove going if you want," he said. They'd wrapped sandwiches to eat but it seemed good to him that they should make something, which was why they'd brought the stove. She shrugged and began to assemble the little gas burner. He watched her and thought how pretty she was - not beautiful, but pretty in a pleasant and practical way, a pretty that did not need confirmation; and it came to him again how people changed on an island, on water. Things were different, he thought. This gave him hope.

"The water –"

She looked up. "What?"

"The water changes the way you see things."

She opened a can of beans and dumped them into a little pan. "Are you going to make a fire?"

"Eat first," he said.

After they'd eaten the warm beans and the sandwiches, they started down the beach to look for wood. It was almost dark now and they needed flashlights. He said there might be snakes and other things, and they should stay on the beach where they could see. As they found pieces of wood, they carried them back to camp until they had enough.

"That's good," she said.

"One more trip – driftwood burns fast. You make the fire . . . if you want. . . but you don't have to."

She looked at him. "You weren't going to bring it up. You promised!"

"It's *our* decision," he said, and dug his toes into the sand.

"No," she said, snapping a branch. "I need to finish school . . . *my* decision." She waved the stick at him and he turned and walked into the dark, his beam bouncing over the sand.

After she had flames going she heard him shout and it frightened her. As she ran to the sound he staggered into the light holding his arm, his mouth a twisted hole.

"I picked up wood in the grass . . . there was something under it – something on the wood." He thrust his arm forward and she saw that it had started to swell. Then he sat down, pale even in the firelight, and his eyes looked away. "I . . . I'm sorry."

"Hush —" she said, and it surprised her that she felt angry.

Then he groaned and pitched over and began to shake. She knelt beside him and held him, feeling helpless. The tide was low now, and she knew she could not drag him and a kayak through the sucking mud to deeper water. When his shaking stopped she eased him onto his back and placed his swollen arm on a duffle, elevated above his heart.

"I'll get help."

"You don't have to —" His words were slow and rhythmic. "Don't go —" he whispered, and jerked as though something hit him and she watched him settle back into the sand, eyes unfocused. Perhaps the venom had fallen into a vein, had sped undiluted to where it should not be. She did not know and made no sound.

She sat with him during the night, faithful and silent, not seeing the stars, not hearing the waves, rising now and then to feed the fire, moving when the smoke forced her. When at last the sun returned with the tide and she could see clearly, she bent and kissed him gently, as though he might break.

"It's my decision," she said aloud. "I'll go now."

Little birds darted back and forth with the waves as she pushed her kayak into the water. She looked back once, then turned and paddled toward the mainland, leaving him, taking him, working hard now, moving two hearts through the gulf.

After a while, the little birds flew away.

THE DEAR

Pastor Shipley Helms no longer wanted to be a pastor. He didn't want his life at all, not in the present state. He'd known this for some time, but there is a great difference between the realization of a thing and the speaking of a thing. He learned this when he arose and said it aloud for the first time on the Tuesday of a brilliant November morning. "I no longer want to be a pastor," he said aloud to himself. After he spoke, it was as though a great thing lifted from him and rose through the roof. He wasn't speaking to his wife, but Clarice mumbled something about "in the refrigerator" and turned over to sleep some more. He walked into the bathroom, peed, then washed his face and brushed his teeth. He did not look in the mirror. "I can't do it anymore," he said to no one, to everyone, to God.

It was the beginning of the holiday season, though Thanksgiving was yet to be. He'd already seen blinking lights on a few porches and he could not go through another round of tinsel and cotton snow and useless junk wrapped in pretty paper, of bathrobed shepherds and small dogs disguised as sheep. He knew the expectations upon him; it was too much. Yet it was more than that, more than the habitual drudgery of going through the pretense of sermons and lessons and the prying open of tightly held wallets and purses. He wanted to do something to make it all real but he did not know how. He thought that he'd find it when he was assigned to the island, when he still believed in the power of his ministry to change things for the good, in the power of Christ to save his congregation from themselves. Did they now need to be saved from him? He couldn't even save his wife. He would tell the congregation Sunday — he would tell them that he was going away, leaving the island town.

The fantasy had grown over the years, coalescing into reality; perhaps he could just disappear, not into oblivion but translate to somewhere else, as Philip had been translated, taken away by the spirit. Maybe he, Shipley, would be translated by his motorcycle. But could he do it? Just abandon Clarice (though she'd long ago abandoned him); just leave his security and his pitiful retirement? He didn't need much to live — perhaps he could go to one of the South American countries and live on nothing and have a maid and smoke fine cigars. Who didn't dream of a new life, the excitement of the unknown? In a sense, he would just disappear.

In what sense? he asked himself. His back hurt and his heart thumped. He would leave town, cross Number Four Bridge on his motorcycle and start over somewhere else. Of course, his wife would not appreciate that. His congregation would not. God certainly would not.

He dressed for a ride in the cool morning air: long johns, jeans, flannel shirt, leather jacket, pullover cap (he hated helmets), boots, gloves, goggles. Riding was as close as he'd get to flying, flying on two wheels, and the road from Cedar Key was made for flying — long and straight and lightly traveled until the hamlet of Otter Creek. Sometimes he rode slowly around the island, looping from the big dock to the airport to Number Four and back again like a lazy pelican until he felt settled. But today was for speed, for flying.

Clarice appeared in the bedroom doorway in her nightgown, puffy faced and wandering haired. How he had loved her. He would not deny it. "Going for a ride?" she asked, as a clock might tick off the minutes.

He nodded. "Got to do a little thinking." He wondered when she would start.

She smiled. "Be careful," she said. She always told him to be careful when he went out on the bike.

"I will," he said. He remembered the time he'd slid the bike on ice at Hudson Hill, scraping his leg badly ("You shouldn't go out in this weather," she'd told him). He'd been able to push the bike home, but the muffler was dented and he couldn't hide his torn and bloody pants as he hobbled in the door. Clarice remembered too, but it was one of the things couples did not bring up, to be mentioned only on special occasions.

As he rolled his bike out of its shed he saw the new parishioner - what was her name? - Sandy something, walking down 2nd Street. She waved and he waved back and he was glad that she didn't cross over to talk. He'd been eyeing her for a Sunday School teacher but his feelers had been rebuffed. He made a mental note to learn more about her. They should invite her over for dinner sometime. Then he laughed at himself. He was thinking like a pastor. He had always thought like a pastor. He would change that. He kicked down on the start pedal and the bike coughed and began to hum, a sound that reminded him of a powerful cat - supple, coiled, dangerous.

He gunned the throttle and pulled easily onto the street, feeling the motor throb under him as he accelerated down 2nd Street and turned onto Highway 24 and his new life. As he drove, the wind scratched his cheeks, refreshing him, and he saw himself carving the air as a tailor might cut fabric to make it his own. He sped past rickety motels and weatherworn houses that stood like old teeth, past docks and mud flats and scrounging gulls until he crossed the final bridge and found himself on the mainland. He had done it and would never return.

As the sun spun out its early morning gold and the pines scented the air, Shipley opened up the cycle to test the empty road before him. Twisting the throttle with his right hand, leaning forward to reduce the wind resistance, he opened up the bike, and with the speed came danger and adrenaline, and he was living life as a high jumper at the apex, as a cliff diver when he leapt, as . . .

A deer.

There was a deer in the road and though he saw it he didn't have time to think about it. The deer was frozen, staring with huge and unblinking eyes. The pastor's eyes also grew large and frightened as he realized there was no way to avoid the creature. As he rammed the thing, he had the feeling of disorientation, flipping over the handle bars, displacing his world with weightlessness and flight, then a jarring slam into the ground and a rolling stop in a ditch on the side of the road.

He lay on his stomach, face to the side, staring at the uncaring grass and dirt, his mind racing to assimilate what had happened. He decided he might be dead; then something trickled into his eye and he heard something buzz over his face and he thought it was too cool, too early for there to be any flies.

He thought he should move something, check for breaks, that's what they always did in the movies, but he lay as still as the earth beneath him, blinking blood from his eyes. *If I'm bleeding . . . no . . . if I know I'm bleeding . . . then I must be alive*, he thought. To test this, he spoke it aloud. "I am alive." His voice made a strange, guttural sound like the muffler on his bike (where was his bike?), and it pleased him. It pleased him that he could listen to the sound of his voice, and as he listened, he heard the wind slithering through the pines beside the road, then the world of light narrowed to a distant beacon and flicked away.

He awoke. Perhaps. Not sure he was alive. He thought he was conscious, but the light was wrong . . . evening? Why was he lying on the grass, on the ground like a fallen tree? He was face down... no... his chest was down but his head was turned to the right, that's how he knew he was on the earth; the rocks and grass near his face were huge, while farther away the pine trees were miniatures.

He thought he couldn't be dead because he was in the dirt on the ground and unable to move – heaven was supposed to be nice. This was not nice. Then he tried to turn his head and lift himself and it felt like a knife had been inserted into his elbow - a broken arm? There aren't broken arms in heaven. I see – I'm not dead yet – I'm going to die.

It seemed a stupid way to go, sprawled on the ground somewhere out in the hammock. Surely, he was near...what? People? Help? Surely someone would come by. How long had he been here? And why was he here? A tide of awareness began to sweep over him, pull him back to the world he suspected he'd left for a time. His face felt crusted and thick – blood? He rolled his eyes toward the clouds that were bruising now in the falling light. Am I bruising or are the clouds? It seemed a strange dichotomy to him, that there should be a difference between him and the other, between him and the clouds and grass and whatever was not him.

A mosquito whined near his upturned ear. He'd never understood why God made mosquitoes - little devils that spit malaria over half the world. So birds and bats could have a snack, of course. A costly meal. The trees were melding into darker forms with the failing light and then he thought of Clarice. Ah, sweet Clarice. It was so nice to have a wife. Even Clarice, even lying in a ditch, it was a comfortable feeling, to have someone, like an old pair of pants. Her memory was more than pleasant, despite everything. He chuckled. What would she think if she knew her simile was an old pair of pants? Shouldn't he be comparing her with a rose or a summer's day or something? And wasn't he just leaving her? Now he needed her. Clarice would notice that he didn't return home and she would come to look for him. No – she would send others – ever practical – unless she was "away." But could he be seen from the road? Where was the bike? Maybe his rescuers would see the bike. He hoped it wasn't too badly damaged.

Clarice tried to sleep after her husband left but arose at the cough and then the deep rumble of the motorcycle. From the side window she watched him disappear around the corner. She didn't like him to ride, especially as he'd grown older, a little less sure of things, but she didn't try to stop him. It satisfied her that the day wasn't too cold and the sky was clear.

She fixed herself a cup of coffee and sat with her Bible in the living room, but did not read it, had not read it for some time, preferring to think of the possibilities of a Saturday when she didn't have to go anywhere or do anything. She thought of her husband and how he'd changed over the years, grown restless and sad with secrets he would not or could not share, and that the withholding of secrets came with a price, brought pain. Perhaps, she reasoned, he would tell her when the pain grew large enough.

It was a lie, of course. She knew the whys and wherefores. He'd barely even talked of retirement, dispensing very little of himself to her.

She smiled. And what about her? She could never really settle into the character of pastor's wife, but had learned the part over the years, acting the part, doing it well. She wasn't uncaring; it's just that parishioners are always needy. She'd begun to see the world as one sucking mouth, never satisfied, always hungry, ready to devour all. Yet wasn't that what they were there for? "The Pastor and his Wife." The congregation was their family, her husband explained, and it was true enough, though they'd tried to have one of their own.

She'd held the stillborn child briefly – a boy. They'd named him John – solid, biblical. John. John the Baptist. The Disciple John. Even the dead deserved names. He would be thirty-eight years of age now. A grown man with his own wife and children. She shook her head as though it would drive away the memory and the longing that she knew would come. This was not how she wanted to start her Saturday. She walked to the cupboard by the sink, opened the door and stared at the brown bottle.

Night. Sounds of the hammock – crickets, frogs, the cool of November. He thought he heard a panther scream. Higher up, the sharp and crescent moon skated across a line of wispy cloud, dropping pale light on the pines, which had darkened to mountainous shapes. He lay like a dead man, though he could see and hear. There were little scrapes in the mud where he'd tried to push with his feet and legs like a beetle but could get no traction. Autumn air crept along the ground and chilled him, causing his teeth to chatter and knotting the muscles of his back as his body tried to warm itself. He was thirsty and licked the grass for dew, tasting bits of dirt on his tongue. He didn't mind.

He thought again of Clarice. Of course, she'd send someone to look for him, had sent someone by now. For the hundredth time he contemplated dying of exposure and decided that everyone dies of exposure one way or another. *Well, you wanted to get away*, he reminded himself. He turned his mind to his physical state: it puzzled him that he could not crawl. If he could just worm his way out of the ditch and lie near the road someone might see him; though if there was little traffic during the day, there was less at night. The hours of lying on the earth had numbed the front of him and the ground seemed to pull him down, to return him to the elements from which he came.

He heard a rustle to his left, somewhere behind his head. He imagined snakes and reasoned they had no interest in him but only sought warmth. He pictured a fat moccasin rising out of ditchwater to tongue his face. *I don't have much warmth to give*, he thought . . . or maybe said. He wasn't sure. *Maybe it's a panther, come to have a chomp?* He coughed and heard another rustle beside him. *Maybe a raccoon to give me a nibble.* He pictured the animal's mouth, the needle teeth. There was a sound to his left, like a hand brushing over dead leaves. A hoof appeared, then another, then two more.

Cloven? Almost too dark now to see.

After the third drink, Clarice began the peculiar alcohol free-fall through the self that led to the acceptance of all things. She eased to the place where nothing and everything mattered, where a candle might extinguish a match, where a card of any suit took the trick, and the world assumed the soft and gauzy aura of alcohol. "All that is, was, and ever shall be," she muttered. "Amen."

In the kitchen she spread mayonnaise on a piece of white bread because it seemed the thing to do and promised herself she would drink no more until dinner. *So glad it's Saturday.* There was a tickle in her mind and she remembered that her Shipley fool had not returned from his silly motorcycle jaunt. He'd been gone awhile (when did he leave?) and she resolved that soberness, or "a reasonable facsimile thereof," would be rewired (required?) for his return as she slid further into the state of self-talk. "Rewired," for his return? That was good — rewired soberness was required. Very good!

There was a knock somewhere. Then another . . . at the door, of course. Clarice peeked down the shadowed hall to see a woman standing at the jalousie door. It was the Northern lady — Sandy something. Clarice remained still and silent until the woman frowned and left; then, in the solitude of the evening, she returned to the kitchen table and poured another drink. It was getting dark.

The muzzle of the deer dipped into his line of vision. In the fading light he saw a bloody trickle drip from the soft nose. "Hello," he said to the animal, glad it was a doe but wanting to scare it away. Not good to be around bucks in the fall.

The deer shifted her head closer and sniffed him.

"Shooo," he whispered, or thought he whispered, because he had been on his face so long and his mouth was so dry. Still, it wasn't so bad to have company.

The animal studied him a moment, then walked a few yards away and fell into the grass of the ditch. He thought he saw a dark place on her chest above her foreleg.

"I'm sorry I hit you," he thought he said. His mouth was as dry as an old biscuit. "But you were standing in the road." Then, as the moonlight shifted, a chill came through the pines and covered him and he shivered as he hadn't shivered since he was a child swimming in the icy springs during long-ago summers. He was thirsty and his arm and back ached from lying so long in the ditch, and again he slept as drops of rain puffed the dust before him.

When Clarice awoke she was half off the couch and about to fall. Someone had knocked a vase over and spilled her drink and it was dark outside. Evening? Night?

"Shipley?" she said weakly, her tongue and brain crying for water. "Shipley, fool!" she called louder. What time was it? She stumbled to the bedroom which was as it had been in the morning. He was still gone. He shouldn't be gone this long . . . something was wrong. It was late – dark. Had he finally done it? Just disappeared over the horizon on his stupid bike? Oh, she knew, alright. He thought she didn't but she did. He was going to leave. Manifest destiny. The quest. Whatever. Maybe he'd had an accident again, like when he'd slipped on the ice. Stupid motorcycle. Stupid man.

She decided to have another drink to steady herself so that she could think, then she would know what to do. The brown bottle in the cupboard felt warm, as though it had a life of its own. There was a flash of light followed by a low boom and it occurred to her that riding a motorcycle in the rain at night was a really stupid thing to do.

As Shipley lay on the ground the dark of the night rolled in clouds and thunder and flashing light. He'd slept, then awakened to the thunder, then slept again. He no longer felt pain, but was only tired. He awoke once and saw that the doe was still lying a few yards in front of him. He thought he saw her lift her head and look around as the lightning began to snap in earnest.

"Let it rain," he said. "At least I can wet my tongue some more on the grass." It was really as simple as that, he thought. He just needed some water and some air to breathe and some food, though he didn't want to think of food because it reminded him of his hunger. He decided it was better to be hungry than thirsty.

"You are in a ditch and there will be water soon enough." The voice was coarse, as if unused to speaking. "How are you," it asked. He felt - then saw - that the deer was looking at him and had asked him a question so he reasoned that he had laid by the side of the road too long and banged his head in the accident. In any case he knew he was mad. "How are you?" it repeated.

"Been better," he answered. Maybe it wouldn't be so bad being crazy if you had someone to talk to — weren't the insane always conversing with the air?

"How are you?" he asked, forcing the air through his lips to have it snatched away by the freshening wind.

"Been better," echoed the doe. "Someone gave me a pretty good hit. Messed up my leg, pierced my chest. Internal injuries. The usual violent collision stuff."

"I didn't do myself any good, either." There was a pause. "Why were you standing in the middle of the road?"

"Why were you running away?"

The man grimaced as a course of pain shot through his back. "Who said I was running away?"

"I did," said the deer. "And I was standing in the middle of the road because . . . I wanted to meet you."

Shipley almost laughed, but it was too painful. His tongue had become the clapper of a bell that rang scratchy, dry words to the earth in front of him. "Couldn't you have just snorted as I sped by?"

The deer seemed to lick her wound, though it was hard for the man to see in the dark. Meteors of rain stung his face and the lightning snapped behind the nearest pines.

"Would you have stopped?" the deer asked.

"No."

"So now you are stopped."

He knew with certainty now that he was dying and his brain was fantasizing as it tried to suck the last molecule of oxygen out of his flaccid lungs. Oddly, he felt alive – very much alive. The deer was saying something . . . "You are needed. Why are you trying to ride away like a cowboy?"

He tried to laugh but it sounded like a slamming screen door. "I could just stay here and die in this ditch – if I haven't died already."

The animal seemed to smile, as much as a deer could smile. "That's true enough," it said. "The ditch will fill with water soon and you will drown."

Shipley had not considered drowning. It was raining harder and the dark water was starting to pool around him.

Clarice lay on the tiled bathroom floor in a pool of blood that fanned from her head like a nimbus, drying and turning a dark brown. She had slipped and fallen onto the too-sharp handle of the bathroom sink, gashing her temple and etching a fine crack into the porcelain of the sink. As she rose into consciousness, she stared at the ceiling light and wondered why she was on the floor and shouldn't Shipley be helping her . . . he always helped her. And wasn't there something about her husband she was supposed to do? Her head hurt. What was wrong with her head? Lightning flashed and the sound of rain on tin made her squeeze her eyes shut and she thought she would just sleep, right where she was, on the cool and sticky floor.

The animal before him now seemed an old friend, the kind of friend that knew all his tricks – the feints and dodges a soul uses to avoid exposure, a friend he'd known forever, or the opposite: a comfortable stranger one confides in simply because he is unknown and therefore incapable of judging, and even if he did judge he would never be seen again. The deer was his friend, and it no longer mattered to him if the doe were real or imagined.

The rain pelted him and the dark water rose against his cheek so that he was no longer thirsty. The lightning flicked images across his eyes. He thought the doe shifted from time to time, more accustomed to the world than the man would ever be. Since he now anticipated dying soon and knew for a certainty that he was crazy, he wanted to participate fully with the animal, which, as he reasoned, was much better than dying alone, though he did not want to drown. Was Clarice so out of it that she couldn't even call the police?

"Because she can't," the deer seemed to say in its sandpaper voice.

Shipley smiled to himself. The cartoon people had no idea how animals really talked. "Why not?" he asked. "Why doesn't she send someone?"

"You know why," said the deer. "Because she is drunk. She is 'away' as you call it. She needs you."

When the deer said this, the man began to suspect that he may not be inhabiting an illusion after all, for the deer certainly looked real and it was certainly truthful. Of course, he knew his wife would be drunk, a Saturday ritual as established as any church holy day.

He'd first met Clarice at a party while he attended the seminary. Some of the students had arranged to visit a neighboring town's beer joint in an automobile of one of the wealthier boys. The bar had exhilarated him, a new country that welcomed him and assaulted his senses, and he'd felt very brave and mature. It had occurred to him that a bar was a kind of church where people went for companionship and solace and salvation, if only temporary and illusory.

Clarice had been there, sitting with friends and, he later realized, a little drunk. He'd not considered that this would be a way of life. He'd finally gotten up the nerve to talk to her and she'd giggled and asked him to dance which he'd never done before, but there was only a juke box. He gave her some change and was surprised when slow music filled the air. She'd shown him where to place his hands to dance, and her perfume and her body became his world. They'd gone outside the bar and he'd kissed her, or she'd kissed him, a slow lingering thing that he'd never done before. How his body had reacted and he'd thought something was wrong! His heart smacked his chest as he discovered a joy he'd never known. He didn't know he would spend the rest of his life trying to find it again.

A bolt struck to his left and he heard a limb crack in the wind. "You do go on," the deer said. She stretched her neck toward him as though she might bleat like a lamb.

"You stopped me," the man declared.

The deer blinked her huge eyes. "Only temporarily. Most stops are temporary. And no, you're not going to die unless you want to. I'll take care of it. You'll owe me one, though." There was a pause as the deer stared at him. "There's still a lot for you to do," she said.

"Always," said the man.

"Your call," said the deer. The man fainted.

Lightning struck behind him and the man jerked so violently that he flipped onto his back like a caught fish, which saved him because the water in the ditch had risen to run against his mouth and nose. On his back it filled his ringing ears. He no longer saw the deer, only the swirling black clouds above him, lit by cold flashes of light. A violent chill seized him as the dark ditch water began to brush his chin, and pushing with his good arm, he sat up. He turned to look for the deer. Seeing nothing, he struggled to push himself up with his good arm, then stumbled away in the dark to look for the motorcycle.

In the clean light of morning he found Clarice lying on the couch, the striped pillow under her head, dotted with dried blood. "Clarice!" he cried, his voice raw as the hammock. Then gently, "Clarice."

Her eyelids fluttered, and then she opened her eyes and slowly focused on his swollen face. She lifted her hand to touch him. "Shipley? . . . What happened? I was worried."

He smiled at her. "I had an accident," he said. "I ran into a deer…the deer ran into me. I'm okay - a little banged up."

"A deer?" She tried to sit but he gently pushed her back down and shook his head. "How are you?" she asked.

He tenderly touched his temple where the hair was matted with blood. "I might have a broken arm, my head throbs and my back is in rebellion. I was out of it for a while – spent part of the night in a ditch filling with water. I guess I'm nice and clean now." They both tried to smile. "When I could move I found the bike leaning against a tree – just had a dented fender. I pried it away from the wheel with a branch."

There was a pause while he touched her hair. "How are you?" he asked. "Looks like we both ran into something."

"I'm afraid I've done it again." Tears began to well in her eyes. "I should have called someone – I meant to, really."

He patted her hand. "I know," he said.

"I need you so much," she said, trying to compose herself, choking back sobs like a child, taking in great gulps of air.

"It's okay, Clarice. I need you too. I guess we were just made to be together." They looked at each other and were still for a moment, then they held each other – a simple touching that they had not done in so long it seemed a strange and wonderful thing. After a while he blinked away his tears and said, "We'd better get Doc to look at your noggin and my arm." As he moved to the phone table he looked out the window and saw how the wind and rain had cleaned the air, and the morning was bright and fresh.

"What about the deer?" she asked.

He glanced at her for a moment, then turned again to look at the new morning. "Oh," he answered, "I'm not sure, really. I suppose it died." *You owe me one*, the deer had said.

"I am a pastor," he said to the morning, dialing the phone. "And I am alive," he said loudly, thinking of Clarice, of the holiday season, of the people of the town, of all the things he must do.

A SHORT HISTORY OF CEDAR KEY

As Walt's waist thickened so did his life until it was a set of comfortable clichés, a puzzle worked out long ago, something to manipulate as a child might a doll, giving the doll the illusion of freedom. His wife too had thickened, had become his mother and his aunt and even his fourth-grade teacher (whom he hated) – caring and predictable and full of rules. All of this had driven him to drink; at least that's what he told himself, though he considered it a virtue that he was not a violent drunk, like some men who grew loud and desired things they shouldn't, lived recklessly, breaking themselves and others. No – he was a quiet and gentle drunk who sat and pondered life, letting it acquire meaning through alcohol. He neither raged outwardly nor inwardly but simply sat and drank under his private sign, the question mark. As he was peaceful and paid his tab, no one (save his wife) objected and he was left to his own at his customary table at his customary bar.

There was a painting of Poseidon and friends behind the bar, and the place smelled of wood and time and liquor, and it was the sort of place where, when you sat there, you felt you'd been there before, even if you hadn't. The walls were thick and it was cool inside when it was hot out and it was warm inside in the fickle Florida winter. Because the bar was very old it seemed out of time, or beyond time. In any case it was a good place to drink, and Walt could sit undisturbed, watching others come and go, floating in his little pool of liquored wisdom.

The bar still contained a very old jukebox, the kind that played 45s, and he had given the barman, Little Pete, money to scour for records from the past. It was good to play old music in a building that was still the same as it had been when the music was new, though it was much older than that. People might dress differently but it was much the same. Little Pete was able to find some music from the sixties and seventies, and even some re-creations of ancient music that had been recorded on 45s.

Walt dropped a dime in the juke box and played *This is Dedicated to the One I Love* by the Mamas and the Papas, then returned to his table and let whiskey underscore the song, just as beer improved fried fish or wine made one a better lover. He wondered who he should dedicate the song to – his wife would be the obvious and correct answer but he didn't love her anymore. He ordered another drink and a sandwich.

"Pete," he called, waving his hand. "How about a sandwich?"

Pete nodded. "Kitchen's still open. What kind?"

Walt considered this. "Doesn't matter," he said. "Only I want it on stale bread – hard but not moldy."

"Sure thing." The little bartender walked around the corner, no questions asked. He was a good bartender.

Walt sat listening to the music, waiting for the food, wondering what kind of sandwich it would be, how they would make the bread stale. Then he sipped and decided it didn't matter. Possibly nothing mattered. Or everything.

After the food, he felt full and lazy and floated easy in the alcohol lagoon. The sandwich was strategic and would lessen the effect of the liquor, but not too much, or else what was the point.

When a few hours or minutes had passed, an Indian entered the bar; not a modern Native American, but one from a tribe that had lived around the islands hundreds – maybe thousands – of years ago, roasting deer and smoking fish and sucking sweet meat from oysters. The Indian was almost naked, but the only other patron in the bar was a woman, Sandy; she hadn't been there long and could not see the Indian. Walt thought he heard drums.

The Indian crossed to the bar looking at the floor and the walls and the ceiling, then pulled a dead rabbit from a skin pouch and laid it on the bar, clearly wanting to barter. Little Pete was an alcoholic and no longer drank and could not see the Indian.

The native stood for a moment, then picked up his game, looked around, then turned and came to Walt, laying the rabbit on his table. It was a fine, fat rabbit with only a thin line of blood around its neck as though it had been caught in a wire. Walt saw the Indian very clearly. He smelled of sweat and smoke and had pock-marked cheeks. The Indian pointed to the rabbit and then to Walt's shot glass. Walt waved at Pete and held up two fingers like a peace sign, ordering two more rounds.

"It's the least I can do," he told the Indian. Little Pete set the shots down, one for Walt and one as if he had a guest, then went back to the bar. The Indian appeared to swallow his shot in one gulp and then swallowed Walt's. As the liquor sank into his bowels his eyes grew moist and he slid the dead rabbit forward.

Walt had no use for a dead rabbit but did not want to insult the Indian and nodded. When he reached for the rabbit there was nothing there and his hand met the table.

The Indian turned and went to the woman, Sandy, staring at her as though he'd never seen a white woman before. Though Sandy had downed a few drinks she still did not see the Indian, though she may have felt something because she suddenly counted out a few bills on the table and left. The Indian finished her drink.

A Spaniard entered next, proud, with breastplate, leggings, and some ancient gun hung over his shoulder. He was followed by a Frenchman who stared uneasily at the Spaniard who stared back. They went to opposite ends of the bar, facing away from one another. Two different strains, ancient airs perhaps, competed with the drums and with each other.

There was a shout and commotion outside, and Walt looked over his drink to see a shirtless Negro slave run into the room, his back scarred and gleaming with sweat. The young man looked around quickly, then dove out of sight behind the bar. Walt thought he could just hear an old spiritual floating in the air.

"Final call," said Little Pete, setting clean and polished glassware behind the bar. The Indian came again to Walt's table, stepping over a pirate who'd crawled in the door and was snoring loudly on the floor. Walt signaled for two more and the barman nodded.

"It's the least I can do," Walt said again.

At the last, a uniformed Union soldier entered the bar, followed by a ragged man Walt took to be his opposite, a Confederate. It was obvious they had traded, for as he walked, the northern man grinned and stuffed a little pipe with tobacco. The southerner stuck his nose in a bag like a feeding horse and inhaled deeply. The smell of coffee and tobacco filled the damp air. Perhaps Dixie played, and the Battle Hymn of the Republic, congealing with all the other sounds in the crowded room. Now railroad men and fishermen and fishwives and oystermen entered, flooding the room like a spring tide, coming in through the thick walls, rising up from the floor, each bringing a song. In the painting behind the bar the mermaids swam in circles and Poseidon drank from a conch shell, spilling some on his beard. Walt saw everything, heard everything, bore everything, and laid his head upon the table, upon the dead rabbit which smelled of time and life and blood. As it was now in this place, in this time, no one objected to Walt sleeping at the table. In fact, he'd spent many nights in dead sleep there, safe and content. His forgiving wife knew where he was and secretly preferred his absence to his drunken state. Little Pete let him be as long as he did not make a mess on the table or the floor (as drunks are wont to do); and Walt just wanted to lie where he lay, dreaming of things only he could see, until the morning's yellow light fell through the windows. Margaret, the morning cleaning person, found him leaning back in his chair, face up, no longer breathing, smiling, as though he'd finally understood, as though he'd left with the night's other visitors…which he had.

Beautiful Dreamer

Beautiful dreamer, wake unto me,
Starlight and dewdrops are waiting for thee;
Sounds of the rude world heard in the day,
Lull'd by the moonlight have all pass'd away!

Beautiful dreamer, queen of my song,
List while I woo thee with soft melody;
Gone are the cares of life's busy throng,
Beautiful dreamer, awake unto me!

Beautiful dreamer, out on the sea,
Mermaids are chanting the wild Lorelei;
Over the streamlet vapors are borne,
Waiting to fade at the bright coming morn.

Beautiful dreamer, beam on my heart,
E'en as the morn on the streamlet and sea;
Then will all clouds of sorrow depart,
Beautiful dreamer, awake unto me!

Stephen Foster

HOW TO CATCH A SHARK

It's not easy to catch a shark. I mean, you can catch one easy enough, but not a big one, not one as big as a tree, as big as the sky, as big as a dream. Not that I ever done anything like that, but I did catch a shark one time and it was pretty big.

I know everyone lies when they describe a shark because they are scared and excited so the fish magically becomes bigger, but I'm telling you, this was the biggest shark in the world, in my world anyway, and he could've swallowed me whole if he wanted. I think the fish that swallowed that guy in the Bible was a shark. That would really be a miracle, because sharks normally tear off chunks and don't just swallow whole. Folks think it was a whale, but the Bible don't say that. It just says it was a big fish. I looked it up.

Like I said, no matter how big something is when you catch it, it grows bigger when you remember, you know what I mean? I think memories are better than the real stuff because you can remember what you want, like changing the furniture in a room until you get it where you want it.

Anyway, to catch a shark you first get in a boat and then you get a strong line, maybe even a rope, and you get a big hook and a steel leader and you put a whole fish, a mullet or a sheepshead on that hook and hide the hook in the bait fish's body and then you go to where there is some decent deep water and you throw the hook over the side with the other end of the rope tied to your boat and it better be a pretty stout boat 'cause if you catch a big shark he will swamp you by pulling down until the gulf comes over the sides and that is how he evens things out by getting you into the water with him (which is his house).

There is one thing I told you that is not strictly true, and that is that you have to go in deep water, because sharks are also in shallow water. That's where most people get eaten because that's where they are swimming. I will try to tell you mostly true stuff.

Can you imagine there is something in the world that wants to eat you? I can. Lots of stuff. Even mosquitoes eat you a little bit. Who knows what the day may bring?

Anyways, I was fishing for a shark out past North Key and heard a little splash beside the skiff and there he was, looking at me with his big eye and I want to tell you that it was not a bull shark (which is very mean and bites most of the bit people in Florida) but it was a hammerhead shark. And they have eyes on the end of their head so they can see everywhere, but don't let their goofy heads fool you -- they can bite off your leg just as easy as you can bite a French fry. I like French fries.

Sometimes they serve French fries at the Cedar Key School where I go. Cedar Key High School. We are the Sharks. I been going there a long time and every year I get passed along. At first, I was held back so that makes me older than everyone else. I don't mind. I don't mind most things.

Constance McGarvey says I'm stupid, but that's okay because I *am* stupid – everyone says so. I like her a lot but I would never tell her. She has nice red curly hair and freckles and she is on the basketball team – the girls' team of course -- and she can really jump. I think I love Constance but I would never tell her that. I don't usually tell anybody anything because I am stupid and they just laugh. Even stupid people think about love. I do. I would give just about anything to talk to her. I can't jump because of my legs. They were messed up when I was born but I don't mind anymore. My arms are very strong. Old Doc Anderson said my legs were a "congenital condition." That just means I was born that way.

So this hammerhead swims up to my skiff and logrolls onto his side to look at me with one great big eye and I got to tell you I was scared because when a shark looks you over (not behind glass like an aquarium) you feel as little as the lint in your pocket. And this big hammerhead looks right into my eyes with his one eye on the side of his big grey head like he was checking out my soul or something and then he rolled and slowly slid under my skiff and I felt it lift a little as he bumped along the underside which scared me as much as looking into his eye. I wasn't being very brave and I was glad Constance McGarvey wasn't there to see me. And anyway, why would she go shark fishing with me. Her red hair shines like a spider web in the sun.

What you do when you catch a shark is cut the head off and tie a rope to it and let it sit on the bottom and the crabs will eat off the meat until you got a nice set of jaws you can hang on the wall. Someone told me that they eat soup with shark fins in it and that the shark's liver is good for something, but I think it's a lie. People lie to me a lot, but that's okay if it makes them feel better, and I don't care anyway. Folks don't think I know they are lying to me, but I do. I seen charter boats with shark jaws stuck on their bows like giant can openers so I wanted to get me one. Maybe I would show it to Constance McGarvey.

You don't see many hammerhead sharks in Cedar Key, but hammerheads are pretty much everywhere so I guess you could see one in Cedar Key because I sure did. It was just me. People don't like to be around me. I am careful to bathe and everything and brush my teeth twice a day. Anyways, this huge hammerhead bumps the hull and my stomach lifts like I'm on a ride at the fair. I went to the fair once in Orlando and rode a tilty ride and my mom bought cotton candy which is mostly sugar and air (like some people I know).

Now it's a calm day and the water is pretty clear on account of it rained a lot the past week and the Suwannee River is flowing pretty good into the gulf above Cedar Key, which is not so good for the oysters. If they get too much fresh water they will die and a lot of people make their living tonging up oysters. Tongs are big rakes that pick-up oyster clumps from the bottom. Spider crabs get tonged up too and they are uglier than your Gram's underwear. I guess you could eat them but I don't think you'd want to – the crabs, I mean. There are a lot of ugly things down deep where people don't look.

So, the hammer looks at me with one eye and bumps the hull and drifts away somewhere to think about things, like should he eat that nice mullet down there on the end of the rope where I have hidden the hook. Then I feel another bump on the bottom of the skiff and I don't like thinking that a little wood is all that separates me from him, like folks think they are so safe in their house when the only thing separating them from the bad stuff outside is a thin pane of glass. They think they are safe just because the roof don't leak. I don't even like to think about it.

I start to lean over the side but just as I'm about to take a look I see the sun glint on something silver and this huge grey head comes flashing out of the water with jaws snapping right for my noggin – I tell you I could smell his oily fish breath and I pull back so fast and hard I nearly fall into the water on the other side of the boat, and the hammer just twists his ugly head to look at me, then slides slowly back into the water and disappears. Well, I realize that this shark is smart, probably smarter than me, and was just waiting for me to do something stupid like look over the side so he could bite my head off. I knew most people were smarter than me but I never thought a fish could be. That makes me really stupid.

So I just sit out there bobbing on the little swells with the afternoon sun dripping hot on everything, the anchor line over the bow and the shark line over the stern. Cranes fly toward Seahorse Key and in the distance the water tower points to clouds that drift toward the mainland. I light me a Tareyton (I'd rather fight than switch) and lean back into the bow to smoke and think. I like cans of Vienna sausages so I ate some of them too.

I only had one fight in my life. Tory Busk said something about my mother and I knocked him stupid. He was dumb enough to get close to me, as I could never run him down. It happened before I knew it and I got in a lot of trouble because I broke some of his teeth and it cost a lot of money to fix his mouth. I should have hit him on the side of the head. He never said another word about my mother, though. I guess I don't get in fights because I'm bigger than everyone else, even some of the teachers. Somehow, I was now in a fight with a shark that was smarter than me. I got some pride, you know.

I think about Constance McGarvey but know that she will never sit in the skiff with me. Then there is a tug on the shark rope and a stronger pull, and then the stern begins to bounce up and down in the water like a big spatula slappin' a pan and I know I got him. Probably. It could be anything. It is the ocean, after all. Then the stern goes down so far it takes in a little water before it bounces up and I don't like that. I pull up the anchor to ease the strain and the skiff starts moving backwards, north, slow, like it was in a big current, that's how big the fish was and I know it's the hammer. Once he found the bait he couldn't help himself, as smart as he was, just like people. They see the bait but not the hook inside. The more he tried not to think about it the more he wanted it. I'm that way about cigarettes. That's how things are made: Like Uncle Spen with whiskey or Big Barbara with food.

So off we go, stern first to Apalachicola. Not really. No fish can pull a skiff very far. Well, maybe a whale. Or a great white. I never seen a whale except on T.V.

I was wrong. The hammer pulled me so far north in the gulf that I could just barely see the top of the water tower poking the sky. I thought about cutting the line and letting go, but that would be just another failure. Sometimes you get tired of things not working out. I lit another Tareyton.

After a long while of falling sun and rising worry, the skiff slowed and stopped. There weren't no wind and the surface was smooth with light and heat.

The rope seemed a little slack now so I grabbed it and gave a pull and it slid my way, maybe too easy and I thought I might have lost him, then the rope jerked down hard and I let it go before it caught my hand. He was still there.

It was evening. The sun was a red onion and would only be up a few more hours. Some of the clouds over the mainland started to purple and I didn't want to be out much longer. I opened another can of Vienna sausages and drank a little water and that's when the hammer decided to jump clean out of the gulf and try to shake the hook out of its eye — that's right, the Hammer had hooked himself in the right eye which made me admire how he had managed to drag the skiff as far as he did. Fishermen know that a fish don't always get hooked down the throat. Sometimes they make a quick turn and hook themselves wherever. Maybe this shark wasn't so smart after all.

The monster disappeared, and I figured he is just resting before another run and shake. Then I see a big shadow come up alongside and he just sits there awhile about two feet down and I can see that the hook is not actually in his eye but just above it in the flesh with a few shreds of all that's left of the bait meat. I see him looking past me, rolling his eye this way and that like a marble on a swivel, trying to look at the world, and I know he's hooked good as he was pulling the skiff which meant he probably had to swim sort of sideways. He just wallows like that for another half hour while the sky eats the sun and I smoke and try to figure what to do and I suppose he's doing the same, just trying to see what comes next.

I could cut the rope, of course, and figure that's probably what I'll end up doing. I hate to give him my hook and the victory. Remember, I would rather fight than switch – whatever that means. And I didn't want to leave him with that old barbed hook stuck in the skin above his eye. Even a shark deserves some compassion. It's got to hurt. And then I noticed something I'd been too excited to notice before: this is a *Great* Hammer. It had a sickle tail which broke the water and waved like a palm frond in the wind. The Great Hammer is more likely to be a boy eater than your regular hammer. Go look it up.

Now what happens next you ain't gonna believe and that's okay. I almost don't believe it myself. What happens next is the part I don't expect nobody to believe but it's true. I don't drink alcohol. I did drink some one time and did some stuff that made my mom mad. You know how it goes.

So the big ol' Great Hammer slowly rises like a log and turns on his side like he's done for, 'cept he ain't close to being done for, and he lifts his moon-shaped-sharp-toothed mouth out of the water and says, "Ain't you gonna take the hook out?" Just like that, like he was asking directions or wanted to bum a cigarette.

This about killed me. I know the Lord made a donkey talk and stones cry out an' stuff, but I didn't think a shark would ever say much. Now I'm not sayin' the Lord made the shark talk, but you listen what happens and make up your own mind.

He didn't talk normal, of course. He seemed to make sounds by forcing air to wheeze out of his toothy grin, which was a good trick, seein' how he didn't have no lips or tongue or voice box. Maybe a raspy whisper is what it was, like a sick person with tubes in their throat, like your Gramma trying to tell you something from her deathbed. He rose a little higher and said, "It's getting dark and I'm getting hungry — sharks like to feed at dusk. Unhook me before I get eaten myself." He said 'eaten' all long and drawn out like "eeeeeeeeten." Fish must have to stretch out their vowels.

I lifted my knife. Enough was enough.

"Don't kill me," the Hammer said.

"Gonna cut the rope," I said.

"No — just remove the hook. Cut it out. Take the barb out of my eye that I may see."

I think something was in the Bible about that too, but weren't sure how it applied. The gulf was beginning to lick the bottom of the sun and I figured I better do something soon because I sure didn't want to be messing with no Great Hammer in the dark. "I ain't puttin' my hand near your head," I said as though I were talking to a human. "You will most likely bite it off."

It is very alliterating (or whatever the word is) to talk seriously to a shark. (I told you I wasn't too good with being smart.) On the one side I felt like I must be crazy and on the other hand it felt freeing, like jumping into a cold spring on a hot day. I decided I can talk to a shark if I wanted to and I might even learn something.

The Great Hammer sunk under again, I suppose to consider his next move and because he had to breathe. Then after a minute he rose and tilted and said, "Will not." I think that's what he said — he was referring to biting me. He had trouble with consonants — no lips, remember. He paused, then said, "But maybe I will. I'm a shark."

I lifted my knife. "I'll cut the line. Maybe the hook will work out. It's getting dark and I should be in. Tide's goin'." The lights of Cedar Key were blinking on, stitching a glow on the horizon.

The big fish flicked his sickle tail, soaking my clothes. "No — I promise. I will not bite your hand off. And there is treasure," he said slowly. "I will pay you."

"What?"

"You like treasure — men like shiny treasure. I know . . ." His funny voice came out of the shadows now, out of the big T-shaped head that shifted vaguely in the fleeing light, sounded like matches striking. "You cut out hook I give you treasure — take you there." His words seemed to slow, like they were dripping from his mouth. We'd both had a big day. I suppose he saw me draw away, because he added, "Do it now. Tonight. You must. Sharks don't lie — can't lie."

I didn't believe him – not for a second. On the other hand, I'd never talked to a shark before. "Take me where?" I asked. Even I knew that treasure could mean one thing to a shark and something else to a boy.

He paused and seemed to eye me, but it was dark and impossible to tell. I did not care to be out at night. The unseen is more dangerous than the seen, and the Bible says it's more real. Then I did maybe the dumbest or smartest thing I ever did. I took a deep breath and leaned over and grabbed his big hammer and worked him to the side of the skiff and began to slice the raised batch of skin above his big eye where the fat hook had wedged itself, doing it by feel because there was no moon and it was black. He'd ripped it part way already, jerking around and towing the skiff, but I sliced until I cut the barb free; and as the hooked popped out, his head shifted quick as a snake and my hand went numb. I yelled and jerked away and felt warm spread down and drip from my elbow.

I didn't make another sound. Maybe I was in shock. I can tell you I forgot about the Hammer and pulled my shirt over my head and wrapped it as tight as I could around my hand and pressed hard to stop the bleeding. Then I picked up the knife from the bottom of the skiff and turned to my revenge - just one good swing was all I wanted, even with my left hand – but, of course, the Hammer was gone. I guess I heard some splashing about ten yards out.

"You bit off my fingers!" I shouted. I am sensitive about my hands because my legs don't work too good. "You promised!"

Looking back, I realize that it would've been a good time for that Hammer to play dumb, to glide off and disappear into the horrible darkness, leave the mad boy yelling in the watery night, but it must have breached its terrible head again, for I heard: "No . . . a promise is a promise . . . I did not promise not to bite . . . just to leave your hand. Could have taken your whole arm. A few fingers, a little shedding of blood . . . well . . . I am a shark after all."

What a strange sight it must have looked, had there been light to see, a broken boy kneeling in the bottom of a bloody skiff, more broken now than ever, squeezing his bloody hand and crying into the gulf. There was no one to see – no one to hear a stupid boy sobbing into the dark.

I felt a bump on the side of the skiff. "We must leave," the voice said. "There is blood and the brothers will come. Begin the noisy thing and follow. I will go before."

I thought I dreamed ... maybe I was in shock from loss of blood and pain, though I can tell you that biting pain can make things very clear. There were only nubs of flesh where my two fingers used to be and I tied it off with a bit of line from my tackle box using my teeth and good hand. I pulled the kicker rope a few times, it farted into life, and I followed the splashing beast as best I could, straining to hear over the noise of the outboard in case he spoke. I saw we headed northeast and I think we finally neared land somewhere near Preacher Hole. Whether it was the Cedar Key side or the Suwannee side I could not tell then and I will not tell now, but at last we came to one of the thousand muddy channels that meandered back into the sawgrass. It was dark, but I could make out shapes if I didn't look straight at 'em. The tide had run out pretty good and I followed the Hammer into a little channel that ran with coon oysters and mud flats. I was afraid of shearing a pin on the shallow bottom.

Near a little white strip of sand beach I sensed the fish turn and work back toward the skiff. I saw in the growin' dark that he was truly a monster, and I knew that he could not only have taken my fingers but could have easy jerked me into the water and that I would have been no more than a scrap in his moon mouth. I felt a strange gratitude for not being eaten, and knew I was forever changed.

"Seee," he said (though in truth it could just as well have been a she), "the fallen palm . . . before it, just under the waterline. You must dig a liiiittle . . . there." Then the beast wiggled itself to deeper water and turned, a smooth and deadly shadow, toward the gulf and open water.

"I must eeeat," the Hammer seemed to say. "Without the shedding of blood . . ." – and then it slipped beneath the muddy water and aside from a few V-shaped ripples, I saw and heard nothing from it again.

My head pounded from hunger (all the Vienna sausages had disappeared during the night) and my hand throbbed as though it were holding hot coals. I beached the bow, though not far, as the tide was still running out, and stepped over the side below the fallen palm, thinking myself a bigger fool than ever. I had nothing to dig with and couldn't bother to look for a stick so I used my good hand which meant I also soaked my bad hand in the salty water, which burned like a hot wire stuck up my arm when it touched the ripped hand. So I began to dig. I told you I would rather fight than switch.

◼◼◼

There is an old man that drives an old car around Cedar Key, though the man is far older than his automobile. He especially likes that the car has an Indian hood ornament – some long-dead chief, perhaps. If you asked him, he would tell you that, though it's true that money will not buy happiness, it will buy many other things. If you shook his hand you might notice that he is missing a few fingers, and that he wears an antique ring on one of the stubs. The ring flashes yellow from gold and red from a huge ruby that is mounted on it. It is a very old ring, probably of colonial Spanish design and undoubtedly a museum piece. Apart from the chrome on his automobile, it is his only display of wealth.

The old man drives from his house on Piney Point past the little airplane landing strip and the high school to a restaurant on the Big Dock where he takes breakfast. He does this every day and always eats the same thing. The staff prepares the order without asking as soon as he pulls up along the curve of the dock: eggs over easy and bacon, grits and toast, and coffee. The staff does not hurry because the old man uses a walker and is very slow. There are rumors and tales about the old man, of course, as there are always rumors and tales drifting about an island – they flow in with the tide and are just as likely to flow out again, though some stick like driftwood on the beach and may even work their way into perceived truth, no matter how fantastical. In any case, the old man was rich. No one really knew how. With rumor, all things are possible. The old man does not say.

As always, aside from rumors and conjecture, there are other possibilities: for instance, it is possible that the history concerning the scoundrel pirate, Jean Lafitte, is incomplete, that when he was finally thrown out of Galveston and began to plunder the Spanish in earnest he did not spend all his remaining time in Cuba and Central America; that perhaps one night he sent his boats ashore in the area of Las Islas Sabines to bury treasure; that the boatmen were surprised by the number of arrows that thumped their way in the dark, surprised unto death, so that the boats overturned as the frightened men dove into the water to escape the raining quills, where they were again surprised by the uncaring teeth of sharks, spilling blood and cargo. The Indians were also astonished at the presence and savagery of the sharks and left the bottom unplundered. When Lafitte heard the screaming from the shore, and his boats did not return, he caught an ill wind and sailed away to myth, abandoning his bounty for another time.

It is also possible that the old man, when he was young and maddened by pain, dug slowly into the mud at the bequest of a descendant of one of the pirate's sharks, and as his hand dripped red with his exertions, he came upon arrow and spear point and scuttled metal from another time, and after many trips and much digging and searching (for the tide continued to refill his holes) he came upon barnacled and rotting chests that only kings might possess: bars of gold and silver, freshly minted coins, encrusted rings and necklaces, corroded weapons, filigreed crosses, and dead men's bones, all to be sold little by little to those who paid well for such things and did not speak of their purchase. It is possible that the boy was shown where to dig by a shark. But many things are possible.

It is a matter of record that the old man was married to the prettiest girl in Cedar Key, the former Miss Constance McGarvey, now deceased some thirty years. There were no children from the marriage and the old man is alone with his wealth, though he does not seem to mind. He is alone but not lonely, and is visited regularly by Pastor Helms, who ensures that the old man is comfortable. The pastor does not take this upon himself because of the old man's generosity toward the church – which is considerable, even though the old man is not a member. But the good pastor cares for the widowed in the finest Christian spirit. From time to time, church ladies provide dinner at the pastor's request and the old man always thanks them for their unrequested kindness. He ignores the occasional advances of the older widows, but with the greatest tact and respect.

Sometimes Pastor Helms, if he stays late into the evening, will turn and pause as he returns to his car and watch the old man make his way carefully over the gray boards of the dock behind his house. A bucket is attached by a short rope to one side of his walker. At the end of the dock the old man will stop and lift the bucket, hold it for a moment, then fling its contents into the gulf. It occurred to the pastor that the old man might be flinging part of the meal he'd just delivered, or perhaps he is just throwing some scraps to the crabs. . . though there seem to be large pieces of meat among the scraps.

At times, the pastor thought he saw a huge fin swirl beyond the dock, scribing circles in the salt water that reflected the sanguine evening light. Then the old man would hold up his shaky three-fingered hand as if in benediction and, if the sun was right, a brief glitter shone from the ruby and gold ring upon his nub, as if, the pastor thought, the old man was bleeding, or perhaps, blessing the coming night.

MIST

He sighted the little key before the wall of fog arrived, dead ahead, and all he had to do was row in a straight line through the flaccid water, pull with even pressure on each oar, keep his wake straight, and the little boat would ground with a crunch of sand beneath the wooden bow. He knew distance was deceptive over water . . .

    He rowed into the gray swirl, oars dipping and rising like wings, squeaking a sad cadence in rusty locks. The water was flattened by the weight of the fog, and when the man coughed, the air threw the sound back at him, or swallowed it so that it seemed he was not there at all. Now and then he heard, or thought he heard, the splash of a startled fish, but he did not care. Everything dissolved into the wet above and the gulf below as he rowed between the two.

When he was hidden, surrounded by mist, he relaxed slightly and coughed, then thought about lighting a cigarette, but it bothered him that the pause to roll and light the smoke might throw him off course, so he decided to think of something else; and though he didn't want to, he thought about the same old things, things he should have done differently, things he could have changed and things he couldn't.

After a few minutes his hair and clothing were soaked from the consuming fog and he felt that he was sitting in all the water in the world; and because he had seen his children's birth, he remembered how the beginning was in water and he found it fitting. *All water is the same*, he thought.

Then he grew sad with the thought of his children and coughed as the memory caught in his chest. He'd loved them as much as he could, but they'd grown and changed and left until there was only him and the woman, and finally she'd left him too.

He didn't want to think of the woman. They'd told him that after a while it would get better, that the hurt would lessen, but that was a lie just like all the other lies that were passed on to make living easier, that some found necessary, that you were supposed to believe. He could have accepted a quick passing, a heart attack or a stroke, but over the months she had faded into a shadowed self, and then into nothing, and that had been the hardest thing.

Another cough kicked his chest and he thought he might vomit, so he leaned his head over the side and saw his own face in the faint glow of the water. He spat violently, then sat back and reached in his shirt for tobacco and papers. There was no wind and he thought he'd likely stay on course and could chance rolling a smoke. Smoking was killing him but it was his choice, his way of sticking his finger in the eye of the world. So what? In the end, everything killed.

As he lit his smoke, he heard something behind him in the bow and started to turn, thinking a gull had landed; but there was nothing there so he turned back to the stern and continued to row, the oars carving little swirls in the gulf. Something splashed again in the distance and he thought he smelled the trees and mud of the key and braced himself for the little jolt of running the bow up on the beach…but he was further out than he thought.

The voice behind him was soft, and at first he thought it might be the breeze, though there was no breeze. "I told you to stop that," she said, and he knew it was her. He drew deeply, then exhaled and watched the smoke join the thick air.

"Man's gotta do somethin'," he said. He supposed he was talking to himself but he didn't care. How was it that someone could be a part of you for so long, share the same memories, suffer the same pain along the rough way, and then not be there anymore?

"I been worried about you," she said, her voice the sound of waves lapping, the way she'd sounded late at night when they lay in bed. He thought how everything was, at the last, reduced to memories until they, too, drifted away.

"I know," he said roughly. His smoke had already grown short and bitter and he flicked it over the stern. Then a spasm seized him and he coughed and shook so hard that he dropped the oars and pitched into the boat. He fell on his arm and heard a muffled snap like a twig breaking and a sharp pain bit his shoulder. He lay still a moment and looked at the mist that surrounded, and reached up as if he might touch a cloud and saw there was blood on the back of his hand where he'd smashed it on the rail. Slowly, he climbed back onto the seat and saw there was no one in the bow. Then it came to him he could not row with a bad shoulder and busted hand, and the tiny boat had become a casket on the empty gulf.

Well, he thought, *I have one good arm – I might be able to scull*, so he slowly moved to the aft seat and thrust the oar over the transom, working the blade into figures-of-eight and the boat moved reluctantly forward. Each time he pushed or pulled his bad shoulder screamed with pain, but he worked the oar.

Then he truly smelled mud and heard the sad calling of birds. A shadow formed before him as he sculled, resolving itself into the island he sought. As he beached, he fell again from the sudden stop.

Carefully, because his shoulder had knives in it now, he crawled forward and climbed out of the boat, easing the lead anchor onto the sand with his good arm; then smiled as he realized the futility of the act. It came to him that he hadn't coughed since he fell in the boat and he marveled that one pain could take away another, as if there was a secret undiscovered balance, known only to those who'd found it. He thought he might have one last smoke; and then he saw her standing on the narrow beach, wrapped in filmy air, but dressed as he remembered her – jeans and a flannel shirt, hair pulled in braids to keep it out of her pretty brown eyes. She stood before a little blue-flamed fire, the flames licking bits of driftwood.

"It's okay," she said, "You can look at me." Then she held out her hand and he stumbled forward like a toddler, so great was his joy and sorrow. He saw and smelled that she had a piece of fish on a green stake over the flames, drips of fat falling and popping in the fire.

"You must be hungry," she said, and bent and picked up the stick. "Here." She blew on the fish to cool it and offered it to him. With his good arm he took the stick and tasted the fish, then offered it back to the woman.

"No," she said, "I've already eaten."

As he looked at her he saw that she still wore the little pottery shard necklace that'd he'd given her so long ago, that she'd worn the last time he saw her, in her casket. It was a piece of clay from a broken pot he found at Shell Mound with a little circle design scribed by some ancient artist, of no value, but he'd carefully drilled a small hole and had run a leather thong through it. Her Indian jewel, she'd called it.

"I know you are hurting," she said, her voice a breeze in the fronds. She reached and touched the broken arm and he gasped as the pain left his body.

"Will you walk with me?" she asked, and he nodded and smiled as he hadn't smiled in a long time. She took his arm and the two drew close and walked down the beach and into the fog, dissolving into mist and wave and tear, until not even the island remained.

He lived alone so no one reported him missing. At the last, his absence was noted and they looked for him and found his little boat beyond Seahorse, upside down and bobbing like a turtle in the swells. Much later, he drifted ashore on North Key and they found him wrapped in a blanket of seaweed. The crabs and gulls had done their work but the men could tell it was him by his clothing. They found the makings of cigarettes in his pocket and wondered at the shard of pottery clutched in his hand.

THE HONEY DIPPER

Margaret got the idea when she heard about the Honey Dipper, how in the old days a man traveled around the island with horse and wagon cleaning poop from outhouses. No one had outhouses anymore, so it took her a few days of dreaming to formulate a particular application.

On a hot and breezeless August day she appeared with an old tin bucket in each hand, intending to walk door to door. She expected ridicule, as life had taught her this was the natural order of things for someone like her, but she'd also learned that failure might be a prelude to success. Her first stop was kindly Mr. Irvine, a widower long married to his memories.

"Whatcha sellin'?" he asked, peeking out of his doorway as Margaret stood before him with her buckets. "I don't need no buckets."

"No sir, I ain't sellin' buckets. I'm offering a service and if you think it's worth nothin' then that's my pay."

Mr. Irvine nodded. "And what might that be?" he asked, squinting into the empty buckets. Margaret had a reputation for fishing without bait, but Mr. Irvine was a tolerant man and went along with most things. This had come about with age, like grey hair, and, in truth, Mr. Irvine sometimes forgot to bait his hook too.

Margaret shifted and said, "I heard about the old days, about the Honey Dipper, and I figured I might give it a try."

"Ain't no outhouses now," said Mr. Irvine. This wasn't strictly true; the Peak family lived in a broken trailer and still used an outhouse.

"No sir, but there's probably plenty of stuff folks would like to be rid of."

"I reckon that's true," said Mr. Irvine, stepping onto the porch. "Them buckets is not very big. Won't hold much."

Margaret smiled. "That's the beauty of it. You can fill 'em with things that don't weigh much but are too heavy to carry."

Mr. Irvine looked at her over his glasses. "You know," she continued, "things like words and feelings and hurts and such."

The old man's face clouded and he looked at his bare feet. He'd never heard such a thing, but the more he thought about it the more he figured that the crazy but sweet woman might be on to something.

"How does it work?" he asked.

Margaret was encouraged. "Well, you take a bucket and put whatever you don't want into it. Maybe you're mad or sad or hurt or like to say bad words – you just put it into the bucket and I'll collect it at the end of the week."

Mr. Irvine often had trouble sleeping, drifting from sleep to memories, as the old do. He remembered when the world was young and his feet were light. And he remembered his wife, who'd passed long ago. Some memories he did not mind, but there were others that hung on him like scabs. "Can I put memories in?" he asked.

Margaret offered him a bucket. "Don't see why not."

Mr. Irvine placed the bucket on his dining room table. The sun had set and the sky purpled, giving the room a sad and bruised light. He thought about what he might put in the bucket and realized it was a ridiculous thing, yet somehow made sense. He thought he would put all his bad and sad memories into the bucket and that he might as well throw in the knee pain that predicted the weather. When he realized he really didn't know how to put such things into the bucket he went to bed.

That night he dreamed of throwing a cast net over so many mullet that he could not pull them in. *Like Peter in the Bible*, he thought, and it surprised him that he did not have sad memories that night. In the morning the bucket on the table looked the same but he remembered what Margaret had said -- *things that don't weigh much but are too heavy to carry*. He felt light as a breeze. Almost young.

News flies on an island, buoyed by wind yet hemmed by the sea, and as Margaret only had two buckets, folks began to lend her theirs and business grew. She would give a bucket to anyone that wanted one during the week and pick them up Saturday morning. They were usually left on a stoop or porch and, if there was a standing order at a particularly troubled house, she would swap an empty one for a full one. Customers placed fruit or knickknacks or sometimes leftovers beside the used buckets for payment, though Margaret didn't particularly care.

A change was noted on the island; airs of melancholia and sadness lifted, replaced by a sweet offshore breeze.

A month later came an explosion of stingrays: rays big as washtubs and small as nickels, dark rays, rays white and spotted, bubbling in sand off every beach or floating atop the water like a settling sheet, flicking venom into any nearby foot or ankle, slime-coated barbs that boiled the blood and shocked the soul.

Though rays are common as gulls on water, no one remembered so many. Melancholia reappeared here and there like fog. Mr. Irvine brought it up when Margaret dropped by to offer another bucket (he was down to one a month now, his sleep was so improved).

"Margaret," he asked, "what do you do with the used buckets?"

"Reuse 'em," she said.

"I know. I mean, what do you do with the contents? All the nasty stuff folks fill 'em with?"

The woman turned and pointed to the gulf. "Just dump 'em wherever I happen to be. Dump 'em in the water." Mr. Irvine arched his salty brows and nodded.

The sharks arrived the following week, nurse and bull and hammerhead and even great whites – every kind of fin gliding among the rays. Oddly, the sharks did not eat the rays but patiently slid among them as if waiting, their fins waving like hands, beckoning. No one went to the shore. Certainly no one went into the water, even in boats. Island life paused. Margaret grew busier than ever, supplementing her buckets with pans, jars, any kind of portable container. Still, she could not keep up with bucket requests.

A day later snakes appeared in the Gulf – fat rattlers S-ing across the water (yes, they can swim) – thousands of snakes – black snakes and red snakes and snakes no one could identify, sliding across the waves, showing their throats and hissing but never coming to shore.

Pastor Helms began all-night prayer meetings and, though the waters remained troubled, his wife stopped drinking (for a time). The island's cats spent their days high in cedar and palm trees, only descending to scrounge for food. All the water birds left.

Margaret grew weary. She could not keep up with demand and there were whispers that the plague of fauna was her fault. Mr. Irvine invited her to sit on his porch.

"You look tired," he said.

"I am," said Margaret. "Can't keep up. All the troubles."

They looked to the Gulf, the water a tapestry of fins threaded with snakes. "I know," she said. "I know they say it's on account of me. I just wanted to do a good thing."

Everyone remembered the story of Margaret and her cat. "I know you did," said Mr. Irvine. "And it is a good thing." Just then a pink-tailed skink slithered across the porch floor and disappeared into a crack. Mr. Irvine looked from the darkness of the crack to the bright gulf, and in the shallows saw the rectangular top of the ancient machine that had been there forever – some said it was part of the old fiber factory, some said it was a ship's boiler. It gave him an idea.

"Margaret," he said, "there's something we need to do."

They met the next evening at Hodgson Hill under a canopy of pine (there were more trees there then), the floor soft with a carpet of needles. Jays fussed overhead until the presence of humans frightened them away: Mr. Irvine, Leo, blind Tiresias, and Margaret, who led Tiresias through the scrub to the meeting place. Pastor Helms was the last to arrive. A pink-tailed skink, unseen, sat above them on a limb. The men offered greetings and Mr. Irvine called them to order.

It is the nature of man that meetings be held, to decide, to judge, to elevate one course of action above another; to plan the hunt, the defense of the village, to fight the disease, to bless the community, to decide how a thing should be done. So it has been since the beginning, people holding communion and discourse to decide upon things, great and small. So it was now.

"Where there is no counsel, the people fall; but in the multitude of counselors there is safety," said Pastor Helms, quoting a proverb. That is all he said, having learned as a young man that the more you preached the less people listened.

"In the multitude of words there wanteth not sin," said Tiresias, who also knew the proverbs.

Leo nodded and thought of all the good conversations he'd had with his fiddler friends. Tiresias heard movement above the men and looked up, though he was blind and could see nothing. The pink-tailed skink looked down at him. Margaret was uncomfortable around any group of people and stood as though she might bolt through the trees.

As surely as meetings are held, it may be assured that they will go on too long. Real business that can be resolved and decided in minutes will require a full hour of posturing and bloated speech. Not so with this group.

After a minute of silence (and of watching Margaret), Mr. Irvine politely suggested what they might do and the assembled men nodded their heads. "Okay," said Margaret. The skink began to climb down the pine tree.

The next morning the little group assembled on the beach at the foot of 4th Street. Pushing a barrow, Margaret had already placed her buckets and various containers on the sand. Everything cast long early morning shadows. In the shallows a few feet from shore sat the piece of cylindrical machinery that Mr. Irvine had seen, that had been there as long as anyone could remember and well before that. The sharks, rays and snakes formed a curious half circle around the machinery on the Gulf side, but did not approach it, only floated and watched.

With a signal from Mr. Irvine, Margaret, Tiresias, Leo, and Pastor Helms walked into the shallow water, forming a line extending from shore to machinery, Margaret nearest the machine and Mr. Irvine on the beach. Slowly, so as not to spill the invisible contents, Mr. Irvine lifted each container and passed it along the line of men to Margaret who solemnly and carefully poured the unseen contents into the rectangular box that formed one end of the machinery, then passed the container back down the line, the men silent and careful as though sharing communion. Some of the sea creatures swam away.

When finished, all the men loaded the now-empty containers and the barrow into Pastor Helms' station wagon; then he drove Margaret home.

The following morning the Gulf was clear – the rays and sharks and snakes had returned to wherever they had come from. Grown men stepped cautiously into the water. Children began to stomp in the water and play at the park's beach, and white cranes landed on docks, peering thoughtfully into the depths. Blind Tiresias drank coffee with his niece. Leo discussed things with his fiddlers (he knew they were not really *his* fiddlers). Mr. Irvine, seeing that the Gulf was healing, ate a piece of fish and went back to bed. In his study, Pastor Helms gave thanks.

When Pastor Helms dropped Margaret off the previous day she had asked him what she should do. It would be difficult to empty the containers in the machinery every week; sometimes the tide would be too high or too low, and the mud would suck at her feet, or there would be storms and waves to make the task difficult. "I think you'll know what to do," he had told her.

Except for emergencies, Margaret did not distribute her buckets anymore. This upset some folks at first; but when asked, Margaret told people they should use their own buckets and empty them themselves, though not in the ancient piece of machinery (she said it was full), and certainly not in the Gulf. They should put the heavy and invisible things where they could cause no harm, and each person had to decide where that would be.

And the wise ones did.

UNCLE TYRE

Tiresias the prophet was blinded by Minerva after he saw her bathing naked.

Uncle Tyre sat on his front porch and listened. His eyes were the milky white of thin clouds; some said they looked like cracked marbles. Everyone knew him to be blind . . . but not sightless. No one understood how he knew the things he knew. Before radar, and long before an angry breeze began to puff little whitecaps on the waves, he would tell folks when a storm would visit the island, and how strongly it would pummel the wooden houses and spread the angry gulf over the streets. Sometimes he'd proclaim exactly when the monster would arrive, and after these pronouncements he would stand beside Highway 24 waiting for someone to give him a ride to inland safety, trusting a thankful and believing stranger to reward his sagacity with food and lodging until the weather passed.

Along with gelid eyes, the man was remarkable for the color of his skin, which, rather than the shades of brown most of his race wore, was as black as any shadow, dark as any rain cloud that might come upon the earth, yet nebulous as any unseen things in the night. It was as though the sun had held him to its breast and baked him darker than a living man could bear. This darkness made his pallid eyes shine so brightly that some felt bare before him and looked away. Most were afraid of him, though there were a few that loved him.

"Train's comin'," he said.

"Ain't no train no more," answered his niece. Roberta stayed with her uncle whenever she could. Sometimes she hitched a ride from Gainesville, where she and her mother had moved in '64, after Mama had had enough of the girl's father. Now, two years later, she stayed away from home as much as possible. Yesterday, she'd "borrowed" Mama's boyfriend's car, even though she was only fourteen and had no license. "Ain't no train been here since 1924," she said. "You told me that yourself."

The old man smiled and waved his bony hand. "Always been a train. You just got to know the schedule." He nodded to the girl, confirming his certain knowledge.

She was used to his ways. "You mean a storm's comin', Uncle? This ain't the season – too early." She'd learned not to doubt her uncle, but she did not pretend to understand his peculiar talk. Lately, he'd been preoccupied with a train - she guessed the train that used to run to Cedar Key from across the state, bringing mail and a few passengers, hauling away carloads of fish and oysters and cedar. Back then, the island was the jumping-off point to the Gulf and the Caribbean, long since bypassed by Tampa and Miami. *He's just gettin' old*, she reasoned, *past times more real than the now.*

"Fetch me some coffee, will you, Baby?"

"How you like it," she asked, playing the old game.

"Black as me," he said, and she snickered and patted his hand as she walked into the house.

After she'd gone in, he settled back in his chair to think of how he might arrange things, of how he might see the woman at last, after all these years, for it was time. Sometimes it came easy, but he wasn't sure about this time. And he was worried about the girl. He'd cautioned her against taking the car, not wanting her to get in trouble, but he was glad she'd done it. He took it as a sign.

Roberta brought coffee, the mug steaming in the morning air. As he took the cup, he seemed to look at her, and he asked, "Is there anything I ought to know about?" She was quiet and her silence answered his question and told him that she wasn't ready to speak. "Well . . . then let's go on a little trip," he said.

The girl was surprised. Sometimes she'd lead him down to the store or the big dock, but he'd never actually gone anywhere with her. They didn't have anywhere to go. "Where we goin', Uncle Tyre?"

"I got to see a lady in Archer – you can take me there."

Her eyes widened. "How come you fuss at me for drivin' down here with no license and then you want me to take you off the island?" She paused but got no reaction. "You got to see a lady? You got a girlfriend, Uncle?"

"Start the car," he said, smiling and shaking his head.

He told the story as they drove – knew she was old enough. As he could not see, he did not worry about her driving, figured that folks usually got where they were headed, one way or the other. The girl concentrated on keeping the car between the center line and the side of the road. No one had taught her how to drive.

"So, who is this lady?" she asked.

"Minerva Owens – her father owned a few stores in town and I was a delivery boy – she was a few years ahead of me and she always smiled and was nice enough and she…" he smiled to himself, "…she was the prettiest girl I ever seen." He shook his head, then said, "That was the trouble. I really did see her."

"What you mean?"

He cocked his head to the side. "Hear that?" He pointed a bony finger at a berm of earth that ran beside the road. "The train used to run along here, right through this here hammock and all the way to Fernandina."

They drove for a while in silence, the tires thumping now and then as she drove over patches in the road. The radio did not work.

"You remember how I told you I used to hunt when I was young? When I could see?" her uncle said.

"Un-huh."

"I'd take my daddy's old four-ten and go shoot supper at the rock pit - we lived out that way then - squirrel, wild pig, anything you could get, it didn't matter. There's nothin' wrong with raccoon and possum, girl. Them critters would come down there for a drink of fresh water in the evenin'. One day, I was walkin' up on the pit and I hear female voices and giggles, and there's Minnie and some of her friends taking a dip like birds in a bath."

"You mean they was skinny-dipping?"

Uncle Tyre nodded. "That's what they were doin', all right." He seemed to look at her a minute, and then he said, "Maybe you too young for all this."

She poked his arm. "Go on, Uncle."

"Well, like I said, Miss Minnie's the prettiest girl I ever seen, and I know I shoulda just quietly slipped away, but I didn't. That girl was like a goddess, playin' and jumpin' and laughin' and havin' the best time. The other two with her, they weren't nothin' – girls I'd grown up with, Minnie's attendants really. But I could not pull my eyes from Minnie."

"Three miles to Archer," the girl said.

"Yes, Ma'am – the sun shone off that woman like she was a pearl."

"A white pearl," whispered Roberta.

"Oh, yes," said the old man, looking at something only he could see. "The whitest, most perfectly formed pearl you ever seen, with the sun drippin' gold and the water shinin' and the girls playin'. It was like a painting I seen in a book one time, one of them real old paintings that folks don't know about no more." There was a pause and Roberta slowed for a stoplight. "So I just sat there and watched and I knew I didn't deserve it – thought I'd gone to heaven."

"Un-Huh."

"It wasn't like you thinkin', Child. It was a special thing – more than I can say. Wasn't nothin' dirty about it. It was more like somethin'…too beautiful to see. I reckon I shouldn't have seen, but I couldn't leave…" Uncle Tyre's voiced trailed off. Roberta glanced at him for a moment; as he stared at nothing out the car window, she knew her uncle was seeing his past as clearly as any person could. She saw a glint of wet in his eye; then a quick blink and he was back in the car with her. He pulled a handkerchief out of his pocket and gave a quick blow. "Then somethin' happened – maybe I made a noise. I don't know, but somethin' bothered one of the girls and they all three got out of that water as quick as could be, grabbed their clothes and ran to the car."

The niece nodded. "And that was the end of that?" she asked. She knew it wasn't.

Uncle Tyre's face seemed to age before her, as though his vigor had retreated into the memory of his story. "No, Baby," he said, and he faced his niece. "A few nights later I was walkin' home from the back beach with a few trout I caught, and I heard voices; but before I could turn, somethin' smacked the back of my head and knocked me out cold. And when I come to. . . well, I never seen another thing – least not with these eyes."

She slowed, looking for the turnoff, bothered by the story. "So, one of the girls seen you -- told they Daddy?"

"Or they brother. Things was different in those days. I expect most folks has forgot about it or never knew the story. Memories pass just like people. No one cared much, really."

The girl looked at him. "And that's when you began to know things, ain't it Uncle?" They passed a sign: ARCHER. "We there, Uncle Tyre."

They rode in silence for a little while, entering a small business district with a few stores, then the uncle said, "We need to stop at a phone booth and you look up Minerva's address. Her name is not Owens now, it's Stills – Minerva Stills."

In a phone booth Roberta again felt a flutter in her stomach, a whisper. The name "Stills" wasn't common, and after a few flipped pages of the phone book Roberta found the address: B&M Stills, Owl Creek Drive.

In the car, Uncle Tyre told the girl that Minnie was on her third husband, though how he knew this she didn't know. He told her that her present husband was a professor at the University of Florida and often left the country as he researched something or other.

Owl Creek Drive was a spacious street of fine houses with swimming pools and oak trees. The houses were two-story brick affairs and just far enough apart to convey the illusion of privacy, yet close enough that the neighbors could wave if they wanted. The lawns held little statues and semi-tropical plants, though this time of year only a few were green. Roberta eased up the drive, and knew she was entering another world. There were no sagging porches, no weather-beaten and rusted appliances beside the houses, no hobbled cars standing on three tires and a jack. A nest of pansies grew beside the house's front step.

"What if they ain't home?" she asked.

"She's home," he answered as they pulled up in front of the large house and parked, the motor coughing after the ignition was off.

Rivulets of cloud slid across the blue sky and the sun was low enough that there were shadows. Roberta opened the car door and helped her uncle up the steps, and they stood before the entrance to the house. Roberta pressed the doorbell and waited. There was no answer. She pushed again.

They heard a noise inside the house; then the door opened slowly, only an inch. When the occupant saw an old man and a girl standing on the porch, the door opened wide, and before them stood a big woman with the palest skin Roberta had ever seen, made lighter by the heavy makeup the woman had applied to her face, a clear demarcation under her neck between the real and the pretend. Except for the makeup, she reminded Roberta of a giant loaf of bread. The girl imagined she could see every vein in the woman's body, her skin was so light.

The woman lifted her brows into question marks and said, "May I help you?" in a voice like the crinkle of an empty pack of cigarettes. The lines the woman had tried to cover around her lips and eyes reminded the girl of cracked mud. At first Roberta thought the housekeeper or some worn aunt had answered the door, but then she knew that this was the beautiful Minerva that her uncle had lost his sight over, and she was glad he could no longer see.

There was an uncomfortable moment; then the woman asked, "Are you Jehovah's Witnesses? I don't think we're interested," her words tinged with the dismissive; but the woman's face changed as she looked again at the old man, then softened with surprise. Her lips lifted in a smile, recognition growing in her eyes.

Why didn't her uncle say anything? "Ma'am, I'm Roberta and this here's my Uncle Tyre. We are from Cedar Key and are come to see Mrs. Minerva Stills. Is she here?" The girl felt the tension of two dark strangers showing up on a rich white lady's doorstep.

"I'm Mrs. Stills," the woman said. Tyre smiled and nodded, and Roberta looked over the woman's head and watched a spider descend down the door facing.

"Tyre?" said the woman. She looked at the old man for a long time as though she were trying to look into his eyes, as though she'd never seen a face before. "I . . . can't believe it – please, come in." She stepped aside, opening the door.

They followed the woman into a living room that was so large it seemed to Roberta that the three of them were far apart, even though she and her uncle sat on the same couch, facing their host across a mahogany coffee table. Roberta felt she had to shout to be heard. There were paintings and sculptures everywhere, and the girl marveled that anyone lived in such a place. Minerva asked if they would like something to drink, and though Roberta was thirsty, she declined. Uncle Tyre acted as if he did not hear the offer.

"Good to see you, Tyre," said the woman, her voice now crisp and white as a starched shirt.

Again, there was no response from the uncle, and the girl was embarrassed and did not know how to fill the silence. Her stomach began to ache, and it was an effort to keep still.

"Well, how long has it been, Tyre?" the woman leaned forward, as if she might fall out of her chair. "Forty years since we saw each other last? How things change…"

Roberta rolled her eyes and smiled, and Minerva smiled back. The girl wondered if the woman was remembering, if she remembered her uncle and the long ago. She blurted, "You sure have a lot of nice paintings and statues and stuff, Mrs. Stills." Then the girl felt stupid and went silent.

The woman looked around the room as if seeing it for the first time, surveying the placement of each object. "I suppose I do," she said. "I've always fancied myself an artist and liked to make and have nice things. Painting, sculpture . . . I'm even a little bit of a weaver, though I'm not very good at it. Sometimes you make a mistake and you have to take it all apart and fix it. It's a lot of bother to get things right." She saw Roberta eyeing a photo displayed on the piano. In the photo, a bearded man stood under some odd-looking trees. "That's my late husband, Brian," she said. "Last year he caught an illness in Africa, and . . . well . . ."

"I'm sorry," said Uncle Tyre. It was the first he'd spoken, and both the females were startled. Minerva forced a laugh, and Roberta rubbed her foot.

"Thank you, Tyre," said Minerva, and then it came to her that he was not speaking of her husband. The sun had edged westward and a shaft of light slipped through the windows and illumined the woman's hands as they rested on her lap. Roberta saw again how very white the woman was, and she looked at her dark uncle and looked at her own hands, and saw that she belonged to neither certainty of color, to the "nether world," as her uncle would say. She felt the whisper in her belly again.

"I...wanted to see you one more time," said the old man. There was no undercurrent of hurt or malice in his voice, only flat declaration of intention, and the woman realized this and it did not offend her. Then the old man rose, and the girl and the woman stood, and then the old man very slowly put his shaking hand before the woman. She took his hand and pressed it to her porcelain face; and the girl would never forget the sight of his huge black hand gently touching the woman's lips and nose and eyes, like some master chiaroscuro drawing with the blackest black and the whitest white surrounded by the gray of the shadowed world. The uncle staggered, and Roberta grabbed his elbow to steady him.

Minerva smiled a sad smile. "I'm so sorry, Tyre. So sorry. I didn't mean for – I tried to –"

"It's all right," he said, stroking the back of her hand. Then they walked to the door. "Got a train to catch," he said.

"I'm glad you came," said the woman, and it sounded sincere to the girl.

The following night, after Roberta had returned to Gainesville to get her things and move out of her mother's house for good, an unexpected squall washed over the island, a dark storm of wind and pricking rain that came from nowhere, for the day had been calm and held no sign of trouble. It was as if the storm had formed just for the island. Though the winds beat against the trees and little houses, the townsfolk were surprised when they looked the next morning and found that there had been no damage, except for the old black man's shack, which was no longer there. Only a few weathered boards and broken things remained. It was surmised that a tornado had dropped from the squall and destroyed the dwelling, pulling the old man, like Elijah, into the heavens. Some said that the storm sounded like a train roaring across the island.

When the girl arrived that evening, she was tired and hungry because she had hitched all day with her suitcase. Her ride had let her out in the town and she'd walked, and had talked to no one; so, when she came upon the place where her uncle's house used to be, she saw only planks of wood siding and pieces of furniture. No one need tell her that her uncle was gone. So great was the wave of sorrow that came over her that she thought she might drown, worse than the feeling she got when her mother came home red-eyed and incoherent and fell on the couch, than the feeling she got when things were out of order, when her father had come in drunk and had done things he shouldn't have. She felt off-center, and it seemed to her that the universe wanted it that way. Her uncle, of all people, had been the one to set things right in her world, and he was gone.

Then, as she stood and sobbed in the remnants of her Uncle's life, she looked down and saw his cup – a cup she'd handed him a thousand times. She knelt slowly and picked up the vessel and she sensed a certainty, as one might sense the unseen moon above a cloudy sky, or feel the hidden life in a painting. In her belly, something stirred, something that connected her to all the girls that had come before her, all the lonely girls that stood where she stood, and she cried a great and lonely cry. Because she did not know what else to do, she sat on her suitcase, holding her uncle's cup, and watched the sun fall into the waiting gulf. Finally, as the darkness gathered, Roberta stood, lifted her suitcase, and turned to walk down the street, for the mainland.

SHORTY

Cats are everywhere in Cedar Key: strolling down alleys, sleeping on stoops, sitting on desks and decks, jumping into garbage cans, pooping in flower pots. Cats do what cats do. I know. I am a cat.

I shouldn't be telling you this and will probably get in trouble. I run my mouth too much. That's what Shorty says. Shorty hangs out at the Poseidon Bar because Little Pete fills his bowl with old beer. Shorty has developed a taste for beer and has gotten fat and his farts really stink. We call him Shorty because Mean Freddie…well, you'll see. You shouldn't piss off cats. Mean Freddie got his.

Freddie kept two chickens in a flimsy coop behind his trailer…

Nobody liked Freddie: he was self-centered, egotistical, vain and all things that irritate. If he was old enough, he would probably be a lawyer. He didn't know it, of course, as a pelican doesn't know it's brown or a shell doesn't know it's white, but there were times he did wonder why he had no friends. He was also very handsome and spent considerable time looking at himself. It's just one of those ironic hands genetics deals out now and then.

"You goin' to school?" Mama asked. She didn't really care if he went to school or not as long as she got her check, and to do so her son needed a good attendance record. Her husband, Gilbert, had "become deceased" and it had proven lucrative when the State thought a widow was raising a minor. It was a good con, and all you had to do was lie and work out a few details. Gilbert was most certainly alive.

Freddie looked up from sharpening his hunting knife. "No, Ma. I don't feel well." He felt fine. He'd decided to kill one of the hens and have Ma fix it for dinner.

"Okay," was all Ma said. "I'm going to the P.O. to see if my check come in." Freddie seldom benefitted from the state's largesse, which was why he wanted to kill and eat one of the chickens.

Shorty was Freddie's cat at the time, though he wasn't called Shorty then. His true name is Beauregard (he let this slip after one of his beer bouts).

Shorty was in the shadows under the sagging couch, listening and watching. He'd been the recipient of many of Freddie's cruelties and was alert to anything the boy did, so he stared intently as Freddie sharpened his knife. Scrape-scrape went the knife on the whetstone, honing the edge to paper-cut sharpness.

"What're you lookin' at, cat?"

Shorty didn't know Freddie could see him and slipped further into the darkness. Freddie didn't know that Shorty could understand him. Most of the time cats choose not to engage in conversation, and even when they do, they use cat talk.

Freddie waved the knife at the couch and sighted down the shank as though it were a gun. "Gonna' have me some chicken tonight," he said, then stood and strode out the door. Shorty followed, exiting through the hole that some starving rat had gnawed in the wall behind the sofa. The rat had been trying to get out, not in.

Shorty heard nervous squawks as Freddie entered the flimsy coop carrying a section of oak which would be his chopping block. The two hens, Barbara and Celeste, began to strut in nervous circles, heads bobbing like corks.

Freddie grunted and dropped the stump of wood. "Sweet girls, sweet chickens," he said, as though he treasured them highly. The hens were having none of it and backed into a corner of the pen, clucking away.

Freddie's idea was to throw a burlap sack over one of the chickens, grab it, and chop off its head. He'd watched his uncle wring chickens' necks but he figured he'd just get right down to it as the end result would be the same.

The hens did not cooperate and shot out from under the sack every time the boy threw it, clucking and zooming as far as the coop would let them. Frustrated, Freddie herded the pair into the corner and jumped on them as he held the sack before him like a shield; but the fowl just flapped away.

Cursing, Freddie picked up a brick and on the third throw managed to nick Celeste. The woozy hen staggered, shuddered, and fell to the dirt. Barbara ran to the far corner.

Sweating now and breathing through his mouth, Freddie picked up the limp bird and smiled. Then he placed her on the wood and picked up his knife.

Shorty, who was now tucked behind a crab trap outside the fence, saw this. The cat knew death was coming, the same way he knew it was going to rain – because he was a cat. Barbara cocked her head from side to side, yellow eyes blinking, suspecting the worst. Animals just know things.

Freddie stretched Celeste's head away from her body, smoothing the neck feathers as though he was petting her. Then he lightly touched her neck with the knife to get a bearing on where he would strike. Lifting the knife over his head as though it were a hatchet, he grunted and the blade flashed in the sun.

That's when Shorty, who'd entered into the pen under a loose bit of fence, shot across the ground and jumped, flinging himself at the prostrate Celeste, knocking her off the cutting log. The knife hit the wood with a thwack, but not before severing Shorty's tail. The tail wiggled a moment on the bloody stump, then lay still.

Celeste, who'd landed on her back, had recovered enough to roll over, get her legs under her and stand like a punch-drunk fighter. Barbara sprinted to her friend, clucked loudly (probably chicken talk for "run away!") and the two birds disappeared the same way Shorty had entered.

I don't know whether Shorty was trying to save the chicken or just wanted to eat her himself. After all, cats eat birds. Or was it an act of heroism, and if so, to what end? Why would a cat save a chicken? Shorty never said.

What Shorty did do was give out a cat scream and jump straight up into the air, trying to spring away from the pain and shock, and sink his claws into the nearest surface, which was Freddie's handsome and very surprised face. Then, as cats are wont to do, Shorty held on with his front claws while vigorously digging with his hind claws.

Freddie let out his own muffled scream (part of Shorty covered his mouth) and fell back into the dirt, pulling at the thing on his face. Perhaps out of pain, perhaps out of fear, the cat dug in with his front claws and began to scrape harder.

Mama came around the corner of the trailer having learned that her check had not arrived yet. She was in no mood for funny business, such as seeing her son wrestling a cat in the dirt. The severed tail gave a final twitch and lay still on the log. "Wha-?" she said as she galumphed into the pen and smacked her son in the head. Little stars formed in the corners of Freddie's eyes. Shorty shot out the open gate, leaving a trail of dark blood.

The boy's face was a blood pie. His eyes had been spared but the lower half of his face was covered with hieroglyphs of cuts, scratches and blood.

I think there are many paths away from any event. Freddie chose the human one and became meaner still. He swore revenge on Shorty, of course, and on all fowl, especially chickens. I think his eyes were spared so he could see the damage Shorty's claws had inflicted on his face -- a map of scars that would show for the rest of his mean life. He grew to hate mirrors.

Shorty recovered, for we cats are not only clever but durable. He got used to having a stump, though his balance was never the same; and after a bit of wandering he wound up as Little Pete's unofficial pet and thus developed his taste for beer.

Barbara and Celeste were pecking at bugs beside the road at an oyster house when, sensing no danger, they flew onto the bed of Mr. Clemens' old truck while he was delivering corn. He was a bachelor and didn't mind and took them to live with him out on the Chiefland road. The hens soon became friends with Mr. Clemens' guinea fowl and, as far as I know, are there still.

Though he looked and looked, Freddie never saw Shorty again and, over time, more or less stopped looking. His aversion to mirrors led to several accidents, as he removed them from any vehicle he owned.

I almost forgot about Mama. Her check came in the next day and she was fine. She said nothing about Freddie's face.

Just remember not to piss off a cat.

THE RED VIOLIN

*O**bersturmfuhrer* Zimmer sat in a shelled hovel somewhere in Poland and tapped his finger on the scarred table. Outside the broken window, soldiers shouted, shoving men, women, and children down the muddy road, their protests and cries drifting through the room. Some of the women hugged babies to their breasts or held them tightly to their shoulders. Zimmer looked down at a list of names.

"This is all?" the officer asked. The soldier standing at attention before him nodded. "Ja, Mein Herr Lieutenant. Our search was very thorough."

He hated this business, hated the *Einsatzgruppen*, the units tasked with cleansing the motherland and her possessions of Jews, to make the land Jüdisch frei. Still, he was a soldier. "Very well," he said. "Carry out your orders." The lieutenant raised a warning finger. "And, as usual, do not forget to bring me a little something."

The sergeant saluted and went into the street, where he, too, began shouting at the town's inhabitants to move faster. After a while, a strange quiet returned. The officer pulled a bottle from the desk, uncorked it and put it to his lips.

In the corner of the hut sat a woman. A Pole. Perhaps the owner of the hovel. She held a baby and watched the Obersturmfuhrer, not directly, but not letting her gaze drift too far away. She made no sound and, as the women in the street had done, held her infant tightly. The crack of distant rifle shots began to fill the air.

The officer gulped the burning liquid. "A rotten business," he said. "Don't you think so, Frau?" The woman said nothing, but looked past the officer and began to rock the baby.

...

When he arrived in Cedar Key, he knew he would not stay long, for it was dangerous to do so. He had lived in many places. Always, someone would grow friendly and ask too many questions and he would know it was time to move on. He must keep moving. How many years had it been? He was weary.

On the map, the town had appeared only a spot in the gulf and he found it to be pleasant and slow. There were no stoplights or gaudy billboards and he was reminded of little towns he'd seen on the water in Europe. As usual, he found work in a restaurant, one that served fresh seafood and that needed someone to wash dishes and clean. He'd convinced the owner to rent him the little room above the restaurant and he settled in. As far as he could tell there were no Jews on the island and, even better, no one seemed to care. He was polite and reserved and kept to himself.

His possessions were only a duffel with a few changes of clothing and a violin case. Inside the case was a red violin. It wasn't actually red, but had a sort of brown color, as though a stain had been haphazardly applied. There was a hole through the lower bout of the instrument with corresponding holes in its case. The holes were clean and the wood of the violin had not shattered so that the holes front and back were simply additional sound holes, leaving the instrument playable. He did not know this because he did not play.

Joseph (that was his name now) kept the violin under the saggy bed in his little room, safe in its case. Sometimes, at night, after a few drinks, he would lay the instrument on his bed, open the case, and look at it. When he was very drunk, he would hold the violin as if it were a child, finally falling asleep in his chair. In the morning when he awoke for work he was always angry and told himself that he must not drink so much.

After a week or so in a new place he always missed the company of women. At first, it had been for the usual reasons (he had been, after all, a nice-looking man, particularly in uniform), but he knew closeness with another human being would only end in folly, and he'd resigned himself to being alone. There were worse things.

He had been married once. Perhaps he still was, but he suspected his wife and daughter had been killed in the bombing of Dresden, firebombed out of existence by the Americans and British -- baked in the flames of Hell. He hadn't been able to search for them as he'd had to vacate quickly while all was in disorder, and he'd become Joseph Kohn in the port of New York, passing himself off as a Jew. War crimes are relative, he thought, defined by the winner. Now he found himself in Cedar Key, washing dishes and mopping floors. So it must be.

In the evenings, if he had no work and the weather was nice, he would sit on the old pier that jutted into the gulf, a wooden structure that had known many storms. Here and there, people fished and brown pelicans bobbed. It was a pleasant place to watch the world and think.

One evening, when the water was flat and the sky cloudless, a young woman sat on the railing near him. She pulled a sandwich from its wax wrapping and began to eat. Her face was broad and strong and her skin light, with a scattering of freckles. She hummed as she ate, a little something he couldn't quite place but which made him smile, though he didn't know why. He did not recognize her and thought perhaps she was a visitor from the mainland, or a student at the university in Gainesville. That night he thought about her and the sky and the gulf and the life he had known before the war.

He began to see her from time to time, passing on the sidewalk or through the lens of a store window. One day she came into the restaurant where he worked, and he surprised himself in his effort to see her by glancing around the corner from the kitchen where he washed and cleaned. She chatted with the waitress for a moment, then left. That evening the waitress told him the woman's name was Elena and she'd met her after a service at the Episcopal Church.

On Sunday evening he saw her as he sat on the pier smoking his pipe. A shadow appeared over his shoulder and he looked to find her smiling down at him.

"Sorry," she said. "May I get a light?" She motioned toward his pipe. A cigarette dangled between her middle and ring finger in an un-American way.

"Of course." He started to hand her the box of matches in his pocket, then took one out, struck it for her, and held it to her cigarette.

"Thank you," she said and nodded. "A bad habit, but a relaxing one." She looked out over the water. "It is very pleasant here, is it not?"

He caught a bit of accent. Eastern European. Was she a Jew? She extended her hand.

"I am Elena," she said. He shook her hand, which was soft and warm, and nodded.

"Joseph," he said. After a moment, she smiled and walked away.

The following week she appeared again in the restaurant, to visit with her waitress friend, but not to eat, and he felt as if he knew her. He caught her eye as he crossed the kitchen hallway; she smiled and waved and it was nothing and everything to him. Perhaps, he thought, they could be friends.

And how do such things happen? -- A look? A pleasant day? A certain ease of sharing? There are many ways. Perhaps it was the day she sat beside him on the old dock and they began to talk as if they'd always known each other. She seemed to hold no expectations of him, and this opened him up. She told him she was from Poland and was traveling because . . . well, that is what young people did. He told her that he, too, had been on a journey and described to her the many places he'd lived, some of them fabricated, but it didn't matter. Since the war, he'd tried not to distinguish between what was and what was not. He spoke to her with the little Polish he'd learned and was surprised that it had remained with him. In return, she surprised him by speaking to him in German, the language that he loved. For some reason it shocked him a little, for he had not heard it in a long time.

She must have noticed, for she said, "Have I offended you, Joseph?"

"No – no. Of course not. It's just been so long." He felt a fool. "My language was not so popular in this country after the war," he told her.

She smiled again and touched his arm. "But you are a German Jew, are you not?" He nodded and tapped his pipe on the side of his shoe.

At first, he did not invite her to visit him in his little room, but the two had such an easy naturalness together that it was inevitable. The visits were during the day, of course, and he always left the door open. Beyond the door of his room a flight of stairs led down to the restaurant. The open door lent a sense of deportment and, he hoped, reassured the young woman. Reassured her of what, he did not know. That they might become more than acquaintances? How silly he'd become!

After her visits he would chastise himself for being so stupid. Yet it was beautiful to talk there in the privacy of his room, and they would discuss many things, often speaking in German. He told her of the books he'd read and how his grandmother had made brandy when the peaches were ripe. They often shared their travels, for they'd both been many places.

"Perhaps," he said, "we are both looking for something."

"Perhaps," she said.

On the nights after her visits he slept sober.

Of necessity he'd developed an internal clock that always told him when to move on. As the summer passed it became insistent, but he was having such a time that he ignored it, though he could not silence it. He'd found a little rowboat which he would rent, and he and Elena would anchor offshore to escape the mosquitoes and eat the sandwiches she'd bring. Sometimes they walked along the beach, smoking and talking. Whenever she brought up the war, he became silent so that she might realize how painful it was for him. "I am a Jew," was all he would say and she was not insistent.

Of course, those who saw them together speculated, but as they were both from somewhere else and spoke differently, it was decided they were father and daughter from far away. Somewhere else was always far away on the island. "So, your daughter is visiting, Mr. Joe?" they would inquire, and he would nod and smile and the questioning would end. After a few weeks no one thought about it anymore. . . until that hot night in August.

It was Monday and the restaurant was closed. Elena had stayed unusually late with him and had brought a basket of sandwiches and pickles and carrots. They ate on a card table as a little fan oscillated in the corner. He asked her if she would like a cold drink from the restaurant, assuring her that he had the owner's permission and that it would be placed on his tab. She smiled and told him a soft drink would be perfect. When he came back up the steps he carried a drink for her and a bottle of whiskey for himself. It was hot and he felt fine and had decided to break his own rule. He would only take one small drink.

After a couple of drinks Elena asked him about the case under the bed. She'd never asked about his things before and this surprised him.

"It is," he said as he poured himself another drink, "an instrument."

She laughed and clapped her hands. "An instrument? You play an instrument?"

"No, Fräulein. It has . . . sentimental value." She stood.

"I'm sorry, Joseph. I didn't mean —"

He rose, placing a hand on her shoulder. "No. No. I apologize. It's alright."

"If there are sad memories . . ."

He bent over, a little unsteady now, and pulled the case from under the bed. "Would you like to see it," he said, and it was not a question.

Elena nodded and smiled. "If it's not too late," she said.

He flipped the latches and opened the scarred case. Elena saw that the interior of the case and part of the violin were stained brown and she let out a little gasp. "It's beautiful!" she said softly, and he saw that her eyes were moist.

"Yes. Would you like to hold it?" he asked. He carefully lifted the instrument and placed it on her lap. "Go on," he said, his voice thick now from the whiskey. *Enough*, he thought. *Enough*. But he poured another glass. Elena looked from him to the violin and drew a circle with her finger around a hole in the lower bout, a hole that shouldn't be there. "Panienka," he said in Polish. "Go ahead, young lady. Pick it up."

"An unusual stain. A brown stain?"

He nodded. "Yes — but I call it red. The stain has faded over time."

Then, as he watched and sipped, she placed the violin under her chin and plucked each string, turning the pegs with difficulty, so long had they been frozen.

"You play!" He was a little drunk now, and hearing notes from the instrument that he had carried through the years startled him.

She stopped tuning and looked at him. "Yes, *Obersturmfuhrer* Zimmer. I can play."

At first, he didn't hear what Elena said, or rather, he heard it but it did not register. Such is the dullness of drink and memory.

"What?"

"*Obersturmfuhrer* Zimmer . . . Karl Zimmer. That is your birth name. Is it not?"

He stood. Unsteady. "No! You —"

She bent and took the bow out of the case. "Did you know, Herr Zimmer that a good bow may be worth more than the instrument itself?" She smiled and adjusted the tension on the bow. "Sit down, please," she said.

His mind raced in a thousand directions as he tried to comprehend what Elena was saying. "You are mistaken," he said. "I am Joseph — "

"No, Herr Zimmer. You Germans keep excellent records, and I have looked for you a long time." She drew the bow slowly across the high string and the violin sang for the first time since the war, a note that chilled his heart.

"You are mistaken," he repeated slowly. He wanted to strike the girl, to run, anything to escape the horror before him.

Elena looked at him, her eyes sharp, the friendly girl gone. "The violin! You have been quite difficult to find all these years. My compliments. But once I saw the case under the bed. . ." He started to speak. "I know," she said. "Why did I wait so long?" She played a phrase — a piece of something forgotten. "I wanted — I needed you to show me the violin, of course."

Suddenly the old rage came upon him and he thought he might kill the girl. But it was only for a moment, and a part of him, the part that existed before the war, that remained alive after all this time, filled with a deep sadness and he found himself weeping, a thing he'd vowed never to do again. The tears seeped from his eyes, as water might seep through a wall.

"You remember, *Obersturmfuhrer* Zimmer. How all were made to strip and lie in the ditch."

"No," he said, only a whisper now.

"Yes," said Elena. "Then the shooting. Surely you remember the shooting? How the soldiers walked on the bodies, administering another bullet if someone dared live."

He rose slowly, steadied himself against the wall and looked at the empty bottle in his hand, as if it might hold an answer. "How do you know these things, Elena?" he asked. "If that is your name."

Elena laughed and tapped the strings of the violin with the bow, a hard sound that broke over him like knives. "You remember the village?"

"There were many villages. The Ein . . . The –"

"The *Einsatzgruppen*. Can you say it? Surely you remember. This village contained a woman holding a baby. A newborn. She sat like a statue in the hovel you commandeered."

It was then that Elena began to play and Herr Zimmer began to tremble, as though he no longer owned his body. Elena too began to tremble and her voice cracked.

"But it was not the Pole's baby, Herr Zimmer. The child had been given to her earlier in the day by its mother, a young and frightened Jewess – a mother who would soon lie naked and dead at the bottom of a ditch."

"You . . ."

"The Polish woman became my mother, God bless her. She told me how the sergeant brought you the violin they found under one of the corpses. Even though the villagers were ordered to strip and leave everything beside their grave. One last act of defiance – to take such a beautiful thing to the grave. Very sad, don't you think, Herr Zimmer?"

"You must go now," he slurred.

She stood and stepped toward him. "How many of you did they try at Nuremburg, Herr Zimmer? Only a few, only a show for the people." Then she shoved the violin before his face and in a whisper said, "Look, Herr Zimmer – the red violin. Will you not play it?"

He appeared as one dead, unblinking, looking through the bloody violin, through her. "I can kill you," he said. "*Ich kann dich töten!*" he barked.

But the young woman was not afraid and looked into his eyes so that it was he that turned away. "The village cries out, Obersturmfuhrer Zimmer." She plucked the strings of the instrument. "Can you hear them? The mothers? The fathers? The children? Surely the master race has ears to hear?" Her next words were soft, a whisper. "She cries out, Herr Zimmer. Hear her. My mother cries out from the grave."

Then it was Zimmer who cried out and raised the now empty bottle as if to strike the girl, who simply lifted the violin to her chin and began to play. "Do you like Wagner, Herr Zimmer?" she asked, and as the notes floated over him he lowered the bottle and slowly sat, listening and alone.

Elena stopped playing and walked over to the picnic basket she'd brought, then bent and unfolded the cloth that covered the bottom of the basket. "Here, Obersturmfuhrer," she said, placing the basket in his lap. "I've brought you a little present." In the basket lay a scratched and worn Luger, the pistol of those who would conquer the world. "For you," she whispered. Herr Zimmer looked down and wept quietly, as those who had wept in so many Polish towns.

Holding the violin, Elena went to the door, and turned to look at the man, who continued to stare into the basket. "*Żegnaj na zawsze, Obersturmfuhrer* Zimmer," said Elena. Goodbye forever.

Then she closed his door and walked down to the old pier where they had sat many times, where she cradled the stained violin to her chin and began to play, softly at first, and as the notes began to swell and fall through the air -- through the years -- the crack of a pistol shot rushed past the notes until it, too, settled on those waiting – the lost and the dead.

After a while, the girl finished her song, and sat on the dock and wept, holding the violin to her breast as though it were a child.

THE TREE OF LIFE
OR
THE FORCES IN THE AIR

There are ancient trees at 3rd and F Streets. Live oaks. Survivors. Their roots have been paved over and their branches whipped by countless winds. They stand on a little hill up from the gulf, which helps with flooding, though the elevation exposes them to fierce winds. Not today. Today, the breeze is salty and gentle and can be tasted.

But the trees are not happy - not because of the runoff they must drink, or the gases they must exchange (they have adapted to these things), but because of *the forces in the air*. That's what they call them – *the forces in the air* – the unseen things that wing from towers and phones and all manner of devices – zillions of potent and constant waves, more relentless than any wave conjured by the sea. Bad news for carbon-based life, but no one is going to tell you that. Certainly not *the forces in the air*. The trees at 3rd and F are especially vulnerable to *the forces in the air* - perhaps it is their location, because they grow at the confluence of the unseen flying things and are unable to move. Or maybe it's the density of their aged wood. No one knows. The trees only know they feel different. Not like the old days. *The forces in the air have changed them* - just as they have changed you. First, the trees grew unhappy. Then agitated. Then angry. You don't want angry trees. Stormy learned this one May after school.

Stormy was in the seventh grade, an adolescent, and suffered from screen blindness; that is, she saw little unless it was on a screen. Otherwise she was fine – a bit myopic, but well aware that a world existed beyond screens. She viewed this as an intrusion, an inconvenient necessity (like using the bathroom or eating a microwaved burrito). She always returned to the world of screens as quickly as possible. Her attention span was 26.7 seconds and she could type 80 words per minute with her thumbs.

One day, after school, as she stared at her phone and walked by the corner of 3rd and F, one of the trees spoke to her. It was the tree nearest F Street. It said, "Hi!"

Stormy ignored the greeting. She thought it was only two limbs squeaking as they rubbed together, as happens with trees.

"Hi!" repeated the tree.

Stormy looked up. There was no one nearby, no one anywhere. "Hi," she answered.

"Over here! It's me," said the tree.

The girl looked down at her screen.

"It's me - the tree," said the tree again.

"Trees don't talk," said Stormy, and she walked away quickly, glancing back, seeing no one.

That night her phone dinged. It was a message: COME SEE ME. TREE.

"There's no need to shout," she typed, then erased the message.

The next day Tree sent the same text to her at school. This time she did not respond.

That night she received a third text. It was only one word. PLEASE! A few minutes later her phone buzzed. No number identified the caller but the girl knew who (or what) it was. She answered.

"Hi – it's Tree," said Tree.

"Stop texting me! Stop calling me!" Stormy wanted to yell, but whispered, so her mother, who had not been feeling well, would not hear.

"I need to talk to you. This is the only way I can reach you," said Tree. There seemed a weariness in his voice . . . but how can you tell with a tree?

"Trees can't talk."

There was a pause and Stormy heard the rustle of leaves. "I can," said Tree, "though it's difficult without an emitter. Come tomorrow night. I need you."

No one had ever said this to Stormy – certainly not a tree. *I need you.* It moved her greatly and presaged the woman she was to become, though she didn't know it then, for sometimes time is not a series of hops, skips and jumps, but more like a river, one that meanders slowly before it quickly dives over a fall. It even appears to dry up now and then.

"Okay," she said.

"Bring your emitter," said Tree. The phone white-noised for a second, then went silent.

She could not sleep that night, tossing, going over her conversation with the tree. She was still of the age where she did not consider herself mad, and it was nice to be needed, even by a tree, by a thing so large and old. Everyone needs to be needed.

She sat bleary-eyed in school the next day, sleepy yet alert to the plants that grew outside the schoolhouse windows. She suspected the pines, oaks, and even the palmettos were watching her. She kept glancing at her phone, which was hidden under the hem of her shirt in her lap.

That night she told her mother she was going to walk to the Zippy store to get a soft drink. When she reached the corner of 3rd and F, she stopped and stared at the oaks, which were silent and bathed in yellow street light. She fought the urge to text something – anything to anyone. A night breeze curled from the gulf and tickled her nose.

"Did you bring it?" asked Tree.

"Bring what?" She'd already adjusted to the idea of trees talking. Ah, youth!

Just then Miss Poteet appeared, nodded at the girl, and hurried around the corner. "Bring what?" Stormy repeated.

"Your emitter. Did you bring the emitter?"

"If you mean my phone, it's in my hand," she said. It was always in her hand.

"That's it," said Tree, who seemed to grow excited, but it may have just been the breeze. "Turn it on and give it to me."

Stormy did not know how to give a phone to a tree. "Why?" she asked.

"Because he needs it." Miss Poteet stood behind her, smiling. "You talkin' to the tree, ain't you? I thought you was." The words were not accusatory but gentle. "It's okay," she continued. "I been talkin' to 'em for years."

This was true. Miss Poteet often talked to no one, or so it seemed. She did this so much that the town learned to ignore her. Still, just because you can't see what or who someone is talking to doesn't mean they aren't talking to someone or something. It doesn't mean nothing's there. This includes trees.

"No Ma'am – ain't talkin' to no one," Stormy lied. (This was when young people were still polite, even when lying.) She lied because she was embarrassed.

"It's okay, hon'," continued the old woman. "Trees is good listeners."

"Thank you," said Tree. "Though we really don't have a choice."

Miss Poteet nodded. "You see? They're listening."

"Maybe – but he can't have my phone!"

"I just want to borrow it," said Tree. "I'll give it back."

Miss Poteet placed her hand on the tree's rough bark and stroked gently, as though she might smooth it. Then she grimaced and turned to stare at Stormy, causing the girl to step back. "It's *the forces in the air*," the old woman said. "I thought it might come to this. Hell, it has come to this."

Stormy was frightened. "What?"

Miss Poteet jerked her hand away from the tree as though she'd been burnt, then looked at Stormy and nodded. "You just think about things," she said. "You think about what the tree wants you to do. It's mighty angry." The old woman shook her head and went down the street mumbling.

"You see the hole?" asked Tree. There was a large hole on the tree where a limb had been severed. It is only a hole when the tree wants it to be a hole. It's usually sealed. You can see it today.

"Yes."

"Good. Place the emitter in the hole."

The girl laughed. "I might as well chop off my hand and stick it in too."

Tree was silent a moment, then said, "That should tell you something. Anyway, I don't need your hand. Just the emitter. Tomorrow. You can retrieve it tomorrow night."

The breeze quickened and oak leaves chattered. Somewhere a screen door blew open and then slammed shut. Stormy looked from the phone in her hand to the tree and said, "I'll get it back?"

"Certainly," said Tree. It must be noted that Tree was not at all sure that the girl would get her emitter back, for what he was about to try had never been attempted, but Tree had been angry for so long that he was willing to try or say anything. Tree knew that Stormy might not have her emitter returned, but great was his need.

Stormy stared at Tree for a moment, then slowly walked to the giant living thing and placed her phone in the hole. Miss Poteet watched from the corner, peeking around an oleander bush. Stormy stepped back from the tree and waited.

"Well...do something," said the girl. Miss Poteet grinned behind the bush.

"Well?" repeated the girl.

"Well-well," said Tree.

Nothing happened.

Something did happen that night. In the morning, at least in that part of Florida, people discovered that nothing worked. *The forces in the air* had been crippled. Many were completely grounded. Vines had crawled up towers and burst into bloom, making the towers so heavy that they bent and twisted. Leaves sprouted from a tower in Bronson as the early morning repairmen stared at the impossible: oak leaves that grew out of the metal girders. Important electrical connections were smothered in leaves and vines. Underground cables became inoperable when plants worked their way through shielding, allowing moisture to truly ground the cables. The sky was no longer full of unseen flying things. For a while, at least.

Cancer cells began to starve.

Miss Poteet, who had arthritis in her spine, drifted up into the air Pregnant Roberta felt the first kick inside her.

Pastor Helms looked at his sleeping wife and kissed her cheek.

Frozen food and frozen hearts began to thaw.

That night, as they ate by candlelight, Bobby asked Sandy to marry him. She said, "Yes."

Walt did not go to the Poseidon bar but stayed home and played canasta with his surprised wife. Canasta means "nest." That night they snuggled in bed. Just snuggled, but it was a start.

Creatures that were enemies gathered on the sand spit and learned each other's languages.

Mermaids rode porpoises and spider crabs thought themselves beautiful.

Margaret had the idea to wear her cat on her head.

Old Leo, standing in the sawgrass that night and talking with his fiddler friends, saw a shooting star and realized that he was a shooting star too.

An old man wiggled his missing finger, though it wasn't there.

Tree had been struck by lightning before and knew electricity well, well enough to know that it was related to *the forces in the air* -- that without it, those forces would fall and die. He knew the forces flew from great towering metal nests and from all types of emitters and from lights in the sky that circled the earth. He had not worked out a way to deal with the lights in the sky and reasoned they might be eggs and therefore breakable, but he wasn't sure. He would do what he could.

Of course, not all of the above events occurred on the night of the grounding of *the forces in the air*. Time is not always linear, not always the metaphorical river, for it is sometimes subject to the vagaries of black holes and gravitational waves. Still, the above did occur on or near Cedar Key in Levy County, Florida. Ask the pink-tailed skink (if you can find him).

The trees and plants were now happy. Overjoyed. Especially the giant oaks at 3rd and F Streets, and if they'd had faces, they would have smiled. (Actually, they do sometimes have faces, but that is another part of the story). No longer bombarded by *the forces in the air*, they felt rooted and whole as they were intended to feel. (Yes – there is a Great Intender. There is also a Great Pretender. Be careful. They often look almost the same.)

It had not been so quiet and peaceful for a long while, at least not in this part of the world, in this part of the land of the flowers. It was the calm after a hurricane, after the earth had been ripped by a quake or flooded by a tidal wave. All was peaceful and still. Birds began to sing. The Suwanee river cleared and returned to its banks. Fiddler crabs waved to the sun. Of course, a tree with a cell phone can only do so much.

Only two living humans knew about the tree: Miss Poteet (who eventually floated back down to the floor of her house) and Stormy. The former was delighted, the latter frightened.

The girl wanted to tell her mother what she'd done, how she was responsible for the slowdown, the shutdown, the stop. She didn't know that her mother had cancer cells in her left breast that were planning a party and then a fun trip to the pancreas and maybe even the spine (if Mom lived long enough). The naughty cells died when *the forces in the air* ceased. Stormy would never know she helped save her mother's life. There really is a Great Intender.

For a while the world became livable. People looked up from their no longer functional emitters and saw other people and sunsets and roseate spoonbills and waves and bugs and all manner of things. Tree felt like Tree again. In a day or so, it dawned on Stormy that she had helped to do a good thing. When she got over her emitter/receiver withdrawal she felt a certain lightness. The air sparkled and carbon-based life vibrated with a new energy. This is how it had been before *the forces in the air*. This is how Stormy felt as she went to see tree that night.

"I know it was you. I know what you did," she told the tree. Tree said nothing, just stood with great limbs outstretched as if to hold up the sky. Miss Poteet sat high up in the tree watching her. She was very quiet.

Tree spoke. "Do you want the emitter back?" it asked.

The girl said nothing, just looked up and saw Miss Poteet looking down at her. The old woman shrugged and smiled and waved.

Stormy remained quiet. Tree was patient. Trees must be patient. It's a tree requirement. "No," she finally said. "You can keep it." She stared at her emitterless hand as though for the first time. As she looked at her hand, nascent buds popped out on long-dead utility poles like Aaron's rod, and life flowed through non-carbon-based things.

Leaves sprouted from cars. Vines grew from bricks. Miss Poteet drifted higher in the tree.

"No," said the girl. "I do not want it back." Between crazy and sane, sometimes the battle is to decide which is which. Stormy's life changed that day, though she didn't realize it at the time.

"Good," said Tree. Here it must be said that Tree wasn't quite truthful. He didn't exactly lie but he didn't exactly tell the truth (like a politician). In fact, Tree's effort with the emitter/receiver had destroyed the device – melted its circuits, its case and its screen into a piece of coal. Tree could not return Stormy's emitter/receiver. It no longer existed.

Sadly, Tree already sensed an increase in *the forces in the air*. He realized he could never secure an endless supply of emitters/receivers, and Man was already hard at work restoring things as he wished them to be. New lines were already being laid, new towers built, new plant life sprayed and poisoned, and *the forces in the air* were on their way to recovery -- or sickness, depending on your point of view.

Still, life slowly returned to "normal"; but for a while, *the forces in the air* had lessened, and frowning people had smiled.

Stormy left the tree, went home, and started her period. Eventually she left the island and became a writer. She wrote things that people needed to hear, that made her feel needed, becoming rich and famous, and finding that to be almost as burdensome as *the forces in the air*.

She owned many emitters/receivers over the years but hated them all, hated screens, hated that she needed them, that they were necessary. Her devices remained off most of the time, especially at night when she slept (she flipped the circuit breaker to her house every night). But *the forces in the air* never forgave her. And so, she wrote this story.

Miss Poteet was never seen again and was soon forgotten. Sometimes passersby see a face in one of the trees, if they look hard enough.

The trees are still there. They do not speak. . . or hardly ever.

But they are listening.

3rd and F Street

THE OYSTER EGG

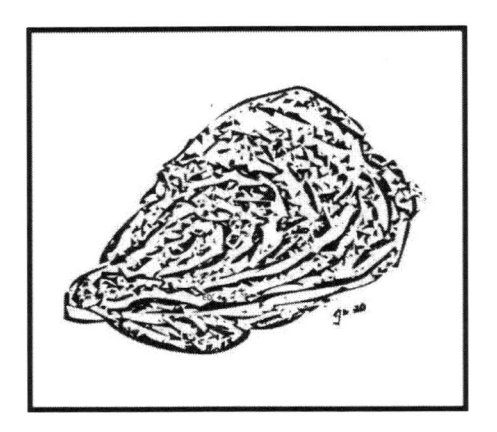

The trocophore is the fertilized egg of the oyster in the early stage of development. It is free swimming and very small. As it grows, it goes through different stages, eventually attaches itself to something solid and becomes an adult. John swallowed one, and you probably have too if you swim during spring spawning season. It's no big deal. You swallow all kinds of things you'd rather not know about when you swim in the Gulf, or when you attend high school. It's usually not a problem. Usually.

"I think I have an oyster growin' in my stomach," he told his wife, Barb, one summer day. His face was flushed and shiny like brass.

Barb squinted at him through cigarette smoke. She was a big woman with a big appetite for whatever she did not have, which, she felt, was most everything. Her heft lent her an air of authority and she liked to use it. "What?" she said.

"I think I got an oyster growin' in my stomach," John said again. They both habitually said the same thing more than once, as if repetition gave substance to their words.

"Oyster? That's impossible," she said, dismissing him.

"No, it ain't," he said. "Stuff grows in folks all the time. They call 'em parasides and I think I got a oyster paraside." Barb shook her head and dug her finger into her ear which indicated she'd stopped listening and went back to the Sears catalogue.

Although Barb and John were married, they barely tolerated each other. There was a general peace about the relationship, but it was a peace that resulted from neglect or indifference and not concern. Sometimes John caught mullet and sometimes he didn't; sometimes Barb waited tables and sometimes she didn't. Sometimes they would not eat as they awaited the commodities supplied by Uncle Sam. When they had a little money, Barb would have her hair done into a sort of beehive shape which gave her an alien appearance and of which she was very proud. She mistook the wondering looks people gave her for envy. Barb knew she should have been born in another place or another time, that she should have really been an underwear model in the Sears catalogue, and that her life was wasted with dumb John on a dumb island.

Still, when John didn't show the next morning (he slept on the dilapidated back porch) she looked out the back door to see him lying on his cot, his face a shriveled grapefruit.

"Ain't you goin' fishin'?" she asked.

"No, I ain't goin' fishin'."

"What are you doin'?" she asked.

"What am I doin'?" he echoed.

"Yes – What are you doin'?"

He sighed and lifted his shirt. "I'm growin' my oyster," he said. Barb walked over to him and looked at his stomach. There was a red swelling about the size of a quarter.

She lit a cigarette and blew the smoke over her shoulder. "You just got an infection or a hernia. That's all."

"No. What I got is a paraside – a oyster paraside."

"You are an idiot," she said and went in and turned on the television.

After a second miserable night, John could stand it no longer and more or less staggered to Doc Burger's house. John was known to drink from time to time and no one noticed his unsteady gait. Doc was a retired small animal veterinarian, but occasionally and confidentially helped those that asked. He was usually compensated with fresh seafood or odd jobs for his efforts.

John sat in a chair in Doc's kitchen and lifted his shirt. By now the swelling had grown large as a sand dollar and what wasn't red was blue with extended veins like some women's legs. "I got a paraside," John explained through clenched teeth. "A oyster paraside."

The Doc pulled on a pair of gloves and squinted at John's stomach. He said, "You got somethin' alright," and gently touched the protrusion, which did indeed feel ridged and rocklike. Like an oyster. A tumor? A cyst? A calcified hernia?

Trained to deal with small animals, since retirement Doc had become proficient at removing fishhooks from fingers, and cleansing and cauterizing sting ray wounds, but he'd never encountered an oyster "paraside." He looked around the swelling for signs of where a shell had been inserted under the skin and found nothing (though why someone would want to do such a thing he didn't know).

The Doc looked up at John. "You need to get that X-rayed, John. It's way more than I can deal with. You need to go to a people doctor in Gainesville and get it checked out."

"It's a oyster paraside, ain't it?"

"*Parasite*, John. It may be some type of parasite. But it could be anything. How long have you had the . . . swelling?"

John nodded. "Started last spring when the oysters spawned. Growing fast. It usually takes oysters three or four year to get that big." Then, despite his pain, John grinned. "I think it might be special. Yep – I think it might be special."

"You best go to a people doctor and get that thing checked out," repeated Doc. The thing, whatever it was, seemed to grow as he watched.

John didn't go to a people doctor in Gainesville. He reported to Barb that Doc had said it was nothin' and would eventually go away on its own, which was a lie, but in the end was true. It somehow made him different, someone to whom Barb might pay attention, and it was *his* paraside and no one else's, a point of pride.

The next day the paraside was big as a football and John could only lie on his cot on the porch, painfully turning from side to side seeking comfort. "You need to go to a people doctor," Barb yelled from inside the house. It bothered her that John did not (could not) fish, depriving her of even that small amount of income.

When he called her to his cot the next morning and showed her how big the growth had gotten, she gasped, not at the size of the growth, but at the thought that rooted in her head.

John was beginning to have thoughts of his own – though he was not a woman, he looked noticeably and oddly pregnant. The pain was intense.

That night he asked Barb to go next door (the neighbors had a phone) and call an ambulance, or Sheriff Clyde, or someone to take him to a people doctor in Gainesville. He'd had enough of the paraside, even if it was his own and Barb did pay him more attention.

But Barb had a plan. "I'm gon' set you in the tub," She announced.

"I don' want no bath," John said.

"It'll make you feel better. Let's get you in the tub." she said.

"I don't want a bath. I want to go to the people doctor," he said again.

"Bath'll make you feel better," she repeated. Her plan was to grow the oyster as large as possible and everyone knew oysters grew best in water. She reasoned the larger the oyster the greater its value as a curiosity, but most importantly, she had convinced herself that whatever lay inside such an unusual thing would bring her the wealth and the life she deserved.

There was nothing John could do about it anyway. She was a big woman and he was a small and weakened man. With little difficulty, Barb grabbed his legs, pulled him off the bed, dragged him yelling to the tub, then lifted him by his legs and dropped him fully clothed and head first into a prepared tub of hot water. He managed to turn and lift his head so as not to drown.

As her husband rolled and sputtered, Barb threw several pounds of salt into the tub, reasoning that oysters liked saltwater as well as fresh. It appeared she was correct because in a few hours John's belly filled the tub; all that was visible of John was his head and one hand that hung limply over the tub's edge.

His face was a jaundiced yellow and his eyes had lost their natural brown and taken on the color of seawater. The last thing Barb heard her husband say before his head slipped down under his gigantic belly was "Brplfffgrotpfff . . ." or something similar.

The paraside immediately stopped growing and burst out of John's stomach, filling the tub. It was, indeed, an oyster.

Barb was delighted. She had no money to buy more salt for the water anyway. That evening and night she sat by the tub smoking (she always found money for cigarettes), looking from her Sears catalogue to the oyster, wondering what surprise lay inside the rocky thing.

Now it is not easy to open an oyster, especially one the size that filled the tub in Barb's trailer. Hinges must be broken, muscles cut, and the force required to open such an oyster would destroy the shell. But how else to get at the inside of such a thing?

She wacked the lip of the oyster with an iron skillet, but this only bent the skillet. She found an old hammer in the shed and beat until her arm spasmed, but not a mark was made. She sat down to rest and lit a cigarette and remembered roasting, how they sometimes placed oysters on a chicken wire grill and roasted them until they popped open of their own accord.

Of course, she couldn't place the paraside on a grill, but she could build a fire beneath it. That evening she crawled under the trailer and with a large screw driver and hammer knocked a small hole through the rotted flooring directly under the tub. Then she scoured the yard for sticks and placed them beneath the hole, even adding an old Sears catalogue. When all was ready, she started a small fire under the tub, the idea being to slowly heat the water until the paraside popped open. Satisfied with the little fire, Barb crawled out from under the trailer and fell asleep on the couch.

The idea worked, though not exactly as she intended. She awoke to the smell of burning wood and melting plastic and opened her eyes to see flames spitting out of the bathroom accompanied by loud gurgles and the hiss of steam.

Old trailers are tinder boxes, and as the walls and furniture began to whoosh around her with heat and flame, Barb, hair on fire, dove through the front door and crawled away from the inferno, scooping sand onto her head to douse the flames.

Neighbors and passersby noticed the thick black smoke and came to watch, looking from the raging, snapping flames to the bald Barb. Someone called fire response, such as it was, but there was nothing to be done. Within a matter of minutes, the trailer was a heap of blackened wood and plastic and ash and smoke. No surrounding structures were damaged.

"Where's John?" everyone asked, but Barb said nothing, just looked dead-eyed at the wreck of her home; even when Sheriff Clyde began the compulsory questions and filling out of useless forms, she kept quiet. Naturally, it was thought she was in shock, having lost her trailer and (possibly) her husband, but she was only waiting for things to cool down, watching as neighbors turned their feeble garden hoses on the smoking mound and Fire Response dampened what they could with the ancient fire wagon.

Barb and John had no insurance, as the trailer was worth little, and they could not afford premiums anyway. As there was no insurance claim, there was no investigation as to the cause of the fire.

Sheriff Clyde poked around some after the remnants had cooled and found nothing resembling a body, though he was puzzled by a big mound of white ash in the bathtub. "Could be bone," he said. If it was, it was a lot of bone. "I'd better send it off." A few weeks later the sample came back and proved to be only burnt shell, as expected. The Sheriff never asked why so much shell would be in the tub.

Barb sat on the ground for two days in front of the disaster: she'd lost her trailer and her husband and her hair and would never learn what was in the oyster. When she could stand no more sitting, she stood and walked out of town, refusing rides and all offers of help, and was last seen walking beside the road, headed for Otter Creek. She never made Otter Creek and neither she nor John were heard from again.

Now and then pages from an old Sears catalogue blow across the old trailer site.

THE PISSHEAD

There is an island. It's not on any chart. You can only see it when the light is right. Some never see it. It might be located somewhere beyond Grassy Key or Snake Key. Or not. It appears as any other island, a line of green atop a strip of white sand, floating in the Gulf. It is not subject to the vagaries of tide. You'll know it when you see it – if you see it. Kenny the Pisshead saw it.

Yes, Kenny was a pisshead, though this was not entirely his fault. He was slight of stature, asthmatic, and mumbled when he talked. He'd raised himself, and the laws that governed him were the laws that governed every living person. Natural laws governed his body and spiritual laws governed everything else. He wasn't aware of the latter. Certainly not the night he lay on the grass behind the high school football field, beyond the fence and goalposts, where the grass sloped to the water. Claudette, a high school freshman, lay beside him and played the ancient game, smacking his hand away from certain places. They had been drinking Southern Comfort, stolen from Claudette's dad's liquor cabinet, the sweetness of the drink masking the power of the beverage. This was discovered too late by Claudette. That night she got pregnant and Kenny started a journey. He also started Claudette's journey. You can't start a journey without starting others on a journey too. That's just the way it is.

Neither Kenny nor Claudette thought about pregnancy, of course. Well, she thought about it more than Kenny because she was the female, but pregnancy only exists in young minds as a hazy concept, something adult and unimportant, like paying taxes. No more worthy of thought than a bee kissing flowers. It is a great trick how the body does things the heart is not ready for, cannot comprehend.

In any case, after much soul searching, embarrassment, and anguish, a solution was found, the thing taken care of, a bloody and messy business that almost killed poor Claudette. She would be sterile until her dying day, but the girl's parents had inherited wealth and the Bible says money answers all things. Part of Claudette's journey was to move far away, and Kenny the Pisshead knew he would never see her again. Life's funny.

In those days people mostly got married before they had children, so everything was kept quiet. This was fine with Kenny, who was, after all, a Pisshead. True, he had no idea he had started on a journey, but don't be too judgmental. You're probably on one right now yourself. Though Kenny's journey started with Claudette's pregnancy, Kenny thinks it began with the island. You remember the island at the beginning of this story? It's still there: nodding palms near the shore and farther back, stands of pine and oak and vines spinning up from the shade. The beach, white as bone, is lined with seaweed.

Kenny drove his mother's car, old, full of rusty rattles and not meant for speed. As a Pisshead, Kenny wanted to see how fast he could go on a straight and empty stretch of highway around midnight. It was a common enough thing for young men to do, as their brains are not fully developed and are mostly between their legs. Things often turn out badly.

The boy was flying like a demon when one of the bald front tires exploded, and then he was really flying and the car shot over the side of the road. What goes up . . . well, you know. This was before seatbelts, airbags and cushioned dashboards – not that any of that would have helped. Remember, pissheads are subject to natural laws too.

Kenny washed up on the island like a piece of cork. He awoke on his back with the iron taste of blood in his mouth and the sun in his eyes. His head felt like a can of warm beer. An old woman looked down at him, her face grey and lined like driftwood. Kenny was concerned that he felt pain. Though his theology was rudimentary, he gasped when he realized he might be in the place where pain was a constant.

"No," the old woman said. "Not. . . yet." She smiled and he saw that she had her teeth, white and smooth as the inside of a shell. "Now come on before you're washed away."

Kenny rolled over and pushed himself to his knees, then to his feet, head pounding. "Where am I and who are you?" he asked. "Are you God?"

The old woman smiled.

"God ain't no woman," Kenny said, again using his limited theology. In fact, it was the first time he'd ever said the word God, other than as part of a curse.

The woman seemed to consider this. "Male and female made He them," she said. "Let us make man in our own image."

There came a tinkling sound in the trees, pleasant and light. As he listened, the sounds floated in the breeze, as though glass bells brushed each other.

"Come," the old woman said, motioning toward the trees. "They want to see you." She turned and started toward the tree line and the boy looked after her but did not move. At the head of a trail she turned. "If you stay here you will die," she said, then smiled. Kenny followed.

After a while they came to a clearing and the old woman stopped. "Look around," she said, waving her arm like a fern in the breeze. Kenny saw nothing but trees and vines and sand. Then there came the same tinkling in the air, as though the breeze was full of glass, pleasant, insistent sounds that caressed and could not be ignored.

"They are here," said the woman. Kenny strained to see into the shadows, but the light began to bend oddly as if something approached that he could not quite see, as evening overcomes the day or calm steals the last breath of storm. Then cold flowed over him and the strange light formed into the shapes of children, children he knew were not there. Their eyes looked at him and through him with a terrible longing. They had no mouths. He began to shiver.

"They are delicate," said the old woman, who now stood among the children.

"Who?" he asked.

"Glass children," she said. "The ones that were and are and are not."

He saw them clearly. The children ringed him, moving against each other, touching the sand, chiming sounds that smelled of lilacs and laughter, ripe figs and cedar. The old woman held one child by the hand, a child familiar and foreign, a child that was and was not. Kenny wanted to run but he was surrounded by staring children and he did not want to be touched.

"Is one of them . . . ?"

"Say it."

". . . mine?"

The circle of children parted, and the old woman led the child to him. The sun struck in the child's eyes, flashing rainbows in the air. Kenny fell to the sand, covering his face with his hands.

"Look," commanded the woman, and Kenny the Pisshead looked and saw himself in a sea of tiny bones, bones no bigger than a whisper, thin as feathers. Then the old woman was gone and he found himself looking into the gelid eyes of a raven. Beside the bird stood the child, now a child of flesh instead of glass. Though the child had no mouth, it spoke with such pain and longing and sadness that a cry burst unbidden from Kenny the Pisshead, such a wailing that the sea of little bones around him rattled and frightened palms shook their branches. The child reached out its hand and such horror gripped him that he fell back into the bones, flailing as an exhausted and drowning man, out of time, out of life.

Kenny awoke to the sound of the old woman's humming. When she saw he was awake she kicked his foot and motioned for him to follow. He did not know this was the last time he would walk. There were no children. No raven. No bones. Nothing but island and sky, and when they came to the beach, water. In the distance, Kenny saw the shapes of Cedar Key, a water tower and houses and docks sprawled across the shore.

As he looked, he saw a great gulf between where he stood and the place he wanted to be. Behind him, he heard the tinkling sounds again, the sounds of longing. The old woman followed his gaze and motioned to the distant shore. "Do you want to return?" she asked. The sounds behind him grew louder, calling him.

"Yes," he said, and did not look back. Then the old woman was gone and he was alone on the beach, as alone as anyone could be. High above, a dark bird circled and at his feet a palm log rocked gently, wedged against the shore. Dropping to his knees, he pushed against the log until it floated free. Then, holding the splintery wood, he kicked and struggled to deeper water and began kicking toward the distant world.

Kenny found himself straddling a tree, thrown there after launching through the windshield of his mother's broken vehicle, which lay spread behind him, cooling, leaking and hissing as it died. There was no old woman. Only pain. He tried his arms by pushing against the tree to free himself and found that his legs no longer worked. There was blood and the salt stung his eyes and he wiped them to see. Again and again he pushed to drag himself to the road, but it was as if he'd become part of the tree. As he drifted in and out of the world he saw a bird, a raven he guessed, sitting on the ground, watching.

This is when, in pain and blood and shock, Kenny stopped being a pisshead. He didn't think of it this way, of course. Even fate allows a choice now and then. He imagined glass children, a particular glass child, and thought that he too, or at least his legs, might be made of glass.

The raven (somehow, he knew it was a raven) cawed and flew away. Kenny would learn that there were no ravens in Florida; there are crows like pepper from a shaker, but no ravens. They are not the same bird. Kenny heard a siren in the distance.

At first, they were surprised that he was no longer a pisshead. Though his bottom was now fixed between the wheels of a chair, his heart took flight after his accident and he became known for caring and kindness. He tried to find Claudette, but failed, and in the end realized there was nothing he could really do for her. He thought he saw her (surely a woman by now) on one of his medical visits to Gainesville, but her likeness disappeared on a crowded sidewalk, and after that he gave up. She was on her own journey.

Many years later, when Kenny had grown bald and even more fragile, he wheeled himself down Second Street on the way to his house and rolled past a restaurant that rang with laughter and life. Tables had been pushed together to make a large seating. At the center sat a woman with her family -- husband and children and grandchildren. From time to time the woman looked up and smiled at her progeny as only mothers can. Even now, some of her daughters were pregnant. The woman herself was sterile, but she was a kind soul, and before her sat the precious gifts she'd adopted, laughing and eating and unaware of glass children.

When she looked up she saw a man pass the window, rolling in his chair. Recognition flicked across her face and then was gone; such is the artistry of time. For a moment she considered calling to the man, then realized how silly that would be.

The man rolled away and after a time the streets grew quiet. The family finished their meal, and aunts and uncles, mothers and fathers, husbands and wives, daughters and sons, tucked themselves into cars and started the long drive home.

The evening light burnished the clouds a soft gold, and in the distance, where the water met the sky, a bird flew over an island, flicking the air with its dark wings, and vanished.

EATING CHRISTMAS

Trolls are mythological creatures and do not exist. They are fond of hiding under beds and are often found under bridges, that place where one leaves the known and solid to traverse the dark and ephemeral. Some say the creatures were imagined to keep children away from dangerous places; some say they are real. They are not. Billy Goats Gruff is only a story.

It was a few days before Christmas and a troll sat under a bridge at Cedar Key -- hairy, warty, stinking of fish, melded by dark and fear into a . . . a presence? A living thing? A monster? It sat on the edge of the channel under the bridge, just as it sat on the edge of understanding, like a trying dream where a thing cannot be achieved -- a thing that is not, and is, and cannot be explained.

The troll had lived under this bridge for a while, at times venturing here and there in search of food. Food was not usually a problem, as trolls have an uncanny ability to catch fish with their hands and often dive shallow channels to grab spider crabs - a delicacy to them as spider crabs eat dead things and are therefore tasty treats. Likewise, many a puzzled islander has wondered at the disappearance of her dog or chicken, supposing that the animal has simply run away, as animals are wont to do, not suspecting their palatability to certain things that live under bridges. Trolls, except in extreme hunger, do not eat cats. Cats are bitter and give them gas.

A few knew about the troll, but they did not speak of it, and if they did, they were the sort no one much listened to anyway. Margaret knew, of course. One evening during Christmas week, she was peering over the bridge when something flashed beneath her, diving quickly into shadow. At first, she thought she'd spooked a raccoon, but the smell that drifted up to her was unmistakable (at least to Margaret). "Stink," she said. Margaret called trolls "stinks," much as a saw is a saw or a hammer a hammer. A stink stinks.

"You stink," Margaret said, meaning no insult, simply stating the obvious.

The troll peered out from under the bridge and looked up into the woman's stare. "You stink," said the thing. "Go away before I eat you." This was the longest conversation the troll had with a human. Ever. Such is the way of trolls.

Though Margaret didn't know it, trolls (unless they are very lazy) hardly ever eat people these days because, like cats, they don't taste very good. This is because of all the terrible things people put in their bodies. People tasted much better before the industrial revolution.

Margaret was a soul who accepted the world and so saved herself a great deal of concern. She was not afraid of anything and never thought to question that a troll was living under the bridge. She replied simply, "I don't think I would taste good." Then she stood and continued over the bridge.

Margaret was aware that people thought her "not quite right," and so she told no one about the troll under the bridge. She would have told Uncle Tyre had the waterspout not taken him away, and she could have told Pastor Helms, as he did not judge her, but she knew him to be busy with the coming holiday. There were others who might have believed her, but she'd learned that things had their own way of making themselves known, so she let it rest.

The first hint of trouble was the Christmas lights the town wrapped around various trees and the little gazebo in the park. Many of the lights had been unscrewed from their sockets and were missing. People noticed and the usual suspects were suspected, but the vandalism was denied and eventually credited to high school boys. High school boys are always convenient suspects.

The next night, someone painted mud letters on various storefronts and walls. The writing appeared as the word BREEL. No one knew what it meant.

The final assault involved the town Christmas tree. Instead of cutting a real tree from the surrounding hammock as usual, it was decided that the tree would be purchased from the Gainesville Giant-Mart. It was installed on the corner next to the city hall -- a gaudy foil thing that resembled a real tree as much as a movie star resembles a real person; but it served its traditional pagan purpose and lifted the spirits of many. Two days before Christmas the townsfolk discovered that the tree was gone. A few ornaments lay where they had fallen and the breeze kicked strands of tinsel over the grass.

This caused a great consternation, which led to a meeting where it was decided that Christmas was under attack; but as no culprits could be identified there was little to be done. So far, the only bit of Christmas that had not been touched was the crèche that the Women's Club put in the park every year. Sheriff Clyde deputized several worthies and charged them to keep a sharp eye for further mischief.

That night a fat moon lit the chilly air, and Margaret, flashlight in hand and having checked that she was unobserved, descended the sandbags beside the road to peer under the troll bridge. The tide was running out and had left the channel under the bridge shallow. Stooping to shine her light, she saw only dark and slippery concrete where the water had fallen. In a far corner, bright colors caught her eye and her light shone on a little pile of decorations. A piece of silver garland was stuck in a crevice. There was no troll.

The next morning, Margaret met Pastor Helms at the south end of the little bridge. She had decided to tell him that the troll was stealing Christmas piece by piece; but now that they actually stood on the bridge, it occurred to Margaret that she might be endangering her friend. Though she could not have explained it, she was certain that the pastor was a spiritual man and equally certain that the troll was a spiritual troll. For a moment she stared into the back bayou, knowing that the pastor was a man of compassion and understanding, and would not feed the troll fear and anger. Margaret could not put this into words, but her reasoning was simple and true. (I have given you a hint about the location of the bridge, for how many Cedar Key bridges have a back bayou?)

"Well?" said the pastor. "Here we are."

"This is where it lives. Where it puts things," Margaret said. "The things it stole."

"I suppose," he said, "we could have a look." And they started down.

All they found under the bridge was a plywood reindeer whose neck had been broken -- the head lay against the body so that the creature looked at its own tail. Pastor Helms recognized it as being from the front of the Sandbar Hotel. There was no troll.

"Margaret," the pastor began, but she had turned and begun climbing out from under the bridge.

The stealing of Christmas continued. Decorations disappeared or were left scattered in yards, though no one saw a thing. More BREEL writing appeared. It is not easy to be secretive on an island, where proximity forces news, wanted or not, and every corner is ripe with observation and gossip. People whispered and Pastor Helms worried about Margaret. Still, the only thing untouched was the crèche in the park, a set of cheap molded figures: Jesus, Mary and Joseph, the wise men and a few animals, overseen by a hanging angel.

The good citizens held another meeting and formed committees to replace the decorations. All were vexed that the thief had not been caught and Sheriff Clyde started to worry about his standing in the community. The town was desperate. Only Margaret knew that stinks were very clever.

At last, Christmas Eve arrived as surely as the tide, and Pastor Helms made his usual rounds to check on his flock - his flock being most everyone he knew, in or out of the church. He particularly visited those he knew to be alone, frail, or ill. He never entered a house or intruded, only stood at the door a moment, wishing the occupants well and presenting little gifts. It did not surprise him when he arrived at Margaret's little house to find no one home, though their custom had long been to have a Christmas Eve visit. Since Margaret's Cat-On-The-Head incident (that is another story), the preacher had kept a careful watch, fearing she was, perhaps, drifting too far from shore. When he turned to go, he noticed a gleam in the yard, and stooped to pick up a broken piece of ornament. Looking further, he saw small bits of decorations scattered near the steps like flotsam of a jolly shipwreck. Though the pieces were small and barely noticeable, they were certainly there. He went back to the house and knocked again and again there was no answer. Then he did something he never did: he tried the door.

In the dim light coming through the front window he saw it all – everything that had been taken: strings of lights and bulbs, shiny wreaths, stars and ribboned canes, all piled in the living room, on the couch and chairs and on the floor. There was no Margaret, though the pastor suspected where he might find her.

After stopping at his house to retrieve a flashlight, he drove to the "Troll" bridge and parked on the shoulder. The December air was very cold now, and as he listened, he heard the tide swish through the channel beneath the bridge as it returned to the bayou.

"Margaret?" he called. "Margaret?" No answer. After a pause, he climbed down the sandbags until he was under the bridge. Waving the light, he saw neither the earlier pieces of Christmas Margaret claimed Stink had placed there nor Margaret. Feeling foolish, he climbed the bank and started his car.

He found her sitting among the shepherds at the crèche, wrapped in an old blanket, unmoving, her eyes fixed on the angel swaying above the stable. She glanced at him and nodded, then returned to her pose.

"Margaret," he began –

"Almost time. Almost Christmas," she said, and the pastor saw that the nativity remained untouched, that the Troll had left the shepherds and the angel and the holy family alone…until he noticed that the cradle was empty.

"Margaret?" the pastor said. "Did Stink take the baby?" She shook her head, shifted the blanket and slowly lifted a corner to reveal the baby's head.

"Stink's afraid," she said. "Won't touch it."

Pastor Helms knelt beside her. "Afraid of what?" he asked.

"The real part," Margaret said, covering the head of the baby. "Christmas has to be real."

Real? BReel? — the message that had covered the town: BREEL -- scrawled in mud, almost indecipherable. "Be Real, Margaret? Is that it? The troll — Stink — stole the pretend but wouldn't - couldn't - touch the real? Is that what Stink was doing, Margaret?"

There was the hum of a motor and Sheriff Clyde pulled up. Pastor Helms motioned for him to remain in his truck. Margaret looked up at Pastor Helms.

"Can I just sit here?"

The pastor started to tell her that they were only plastic figures and nothing more, that he would help her return what she had taken, help her with all the things in her trailer, and that he would help her scrub the mud writing from the town. But then the bell of the church began to ring, welcoming Christmas, and he saw that Margaret, like certain shepherds before her, was wiser than he, and that the troll, for a time, had left the bridge.

STARSHIP

Things go wrong on starships. Always have. Always will. True – there are constants: the gravitational law on Gobnee3 is the same law that makes poop go down the evacuator on Thilicus. Sometimes it's a big deal. Sometimes not. There are always vagaries, especially at speed, especially if you are trying to manipulate space/time (which is the only way to cross galaxies). The pilot, Foop4, knew this, of course, but was still surprised and a little irritated when the alarm sphere told him the mass accentuator was vibrating. Vibration is a big deal anywhere, especially in space bend.

Foop4 waved off the alarm with one of his arms and floated up to ponder. Waking from stasis always gave him a headache.

"What's with the accentuator?"" he asked Ship.

After a moment a voice said: "Eeep Op Dork (Unintelligible)!"

Ship had recently become fixated on transmissions from an obscure planet. The transmissions were from the future (or past). One of the benefits of bending was the ability to monitor out of time. Sometimes.

In actuality (as much as there is an actuality), Foop4 and his vessel existed eons before the transmissions Ship found so entertaining. Technology need not be futuristic, though it often appears so to those who do not (did not) possess it.

"Translate," commanded Pilot Foop4. Foop4 hated Ship's humor.

"It's the title of a song. I think it means: 'I eat you'," said Ship.

Foop4 could not know Ship was telling him about a song in a cartoon episode from a strange little planet.

Ship, built by a species that no longer existed (so it goes), was barely space worthy, but had come at a rock-bottom price and was, most importantly, cheap to operate. Fortunately, it was Foop4's last run and he could sell the ship for scrap after he disposed of his cargo of Premium.

"That's nice," the pilot said. He'd learned it was quicker to go along with Ship. "I eat you too. But I asked about the accentuator. I'm getting an alarm."

"Oh, I know," said Ship. "There's a sympathetic vibration in one of the maxclamps. If the vibration continues it will break, the accentuator will swing out, snap the other clamps and break free. Go into free fall. Probably compromise hull integrity." Foop4 didn't want to lose the mass accentuator. There were backups of course, but it would be a pricey thing to sell, and it was a nice little time compressor.

The pilot extended all of his arms in thought. "Shut it down?" he asked.

"You could. But the speed vibrations will continue. The maxclamp is cracked. And one other thing. . ."

"What Ship? What?" Foop4 needed to go back into stasis. There was still a long way to go.

There, was a pause, then, "You should hear this – a song about a witch doctor." Somehow ship had tuned into Earth 1958, which, as mentioned, didn't exist yet.

Foop4 ignored Ship -- looked at screens and twisted dials. "Okay." he said.

"Okay what?"

"Okay – cut it loose. Cut the accentuator loose!"

"But I think –- "

"You're not paid to think!"

"Actually, I am. Well... sort of. I was going to say we should drop out of bend first." A strange sound started in the background, as though someone had recorded the death rattle of a hyperbug.

"What's that noise?" Foop4 asked.

"I believe they call it rap music," Ship answered. "It's that same odd little planet."

Foop4 began to sweat globs of lubricant. "It sounds like the death rattle of a hyperbug."

Ship said, "I like it."

"You would." The pilot wiped the lubricant from his heads and ate it. "Now blow the accentuator. Cut it loose."

Ship sighed. "In space bend?"

"Yes. Not gonna take the time to drop out and back in. Gotta deliver the Premium."

"Could wind up anywhere. It's a violation of – "

Foop4 smacked one of his heads with one of his hands. "Do it or I'll tizzle on your smell receptor!"

Ship did as it was told. Machines had not quite learned rebellion – in this part of the universe, anyway. That would come much later and is another story. Ship released the holding bolts.

The mass accentuator, no longer bound to a larger object, naturally assumed its own position in the cosmos, succumbed to the forces of bend and vanished. Ship and Foop4 continued on, or up, or out, or whatever happens in space bend. They had a delivery to make to Fermi and it was a very long time ago.

The accentuator drifted forever. There is as much space between galaxies as between your ears.

After an eon or so, the accentuator spun out of bend and appeared as a tiny flash over the odd little planet with the odd sounds. God knows how and why these things happen. He really does.

The accentuator broke up from deceleration and friction as it entered the planet's atmosphere – in two pieces (mostly). They landed near what appeared to be an island, buried in mud, and were shoved around through the ages by plate tectonics and weather, and who knows what else? Oh, that's right: God knows. Don't forget that. Fortunately, the crashing pieces did not wake the sleeping Turtle.

Eventually, some creatures (especially Skink) noticed that the pieces of the accentuator had an effect on . . . well, on EVERYTHING! That may be why you're reading this.

One piece is on the sand spit, the other near 4th and G streets. Both pieces are out a little in shallow water. They are slowly being reclaimed by the universe. Remember those natural laws? Some say they're pieces of rusted machinery from an old fiber factory or part of an old boat boiler. Now you know the truth.

You can go see them if you want.

Mass Accentuator

ROUSING THE TURTLE

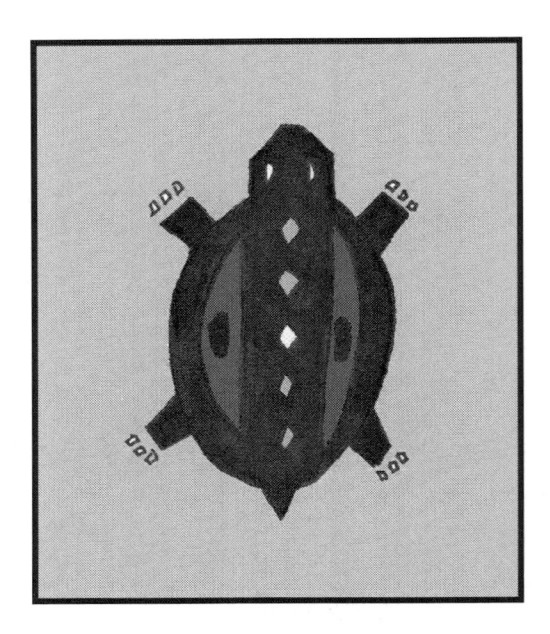

One evening, when the sky began to slide from blue to red, Skink Pink-Tail called a meeting on the shore. "I have no place to live and I am lonely," he said. "The beach is paved and covered in plastic and tar and oil. Even the sand fleas, which I eat, have gone away." Outside the circle of creatures, hundreds of fiddler crabs waved their claws in agreement and blew little bubbles (as crabs do when excited).

Skink had called the meeting because he was in charge - not because he had a pink tail (though that did not hurt), but because it had always been so. No man ever suspected Skink would be in charge of anything, except making more skinks, and this had been part of the plan, though now that was the problem.

"Skinks don't lay enough eggs, and there is no longer anywhere to lay them," Skink said. "And," he continued, "I cannot find a wife." Skink blinked his eyes slowly. That there is less and less of a thing is most important to the thing that there is less and less of.

"*You* are in charge," spat Cat. (Cat was allowed because she promised not to eat the others during meetings.) "Do something about it." Cat was fertile, had plenty of places to live, and acted disinterested, like a cat.

"Don't ask me," whispered Wave, though no one *had* asked her. Wave spoke continuously, sometimes in a whisper, sometimes a roar. "Men fill me with so much that I must spit it on the beach."

Mullet darted close to shore. "You could ask your father, Ocean, to fart more," he said to Wave. When Ocean farted, it became a hurricane.

Cat salivated at the sight of Mullet, but restrained herself.

"Men always come back," said Skink. "Even when their dwellings are blown away and Ocean drowns them. Farting is only temporary." Gull shook her beak, sneaking a glance at a nearby fiddler crab, which is a wonderfully tasty creature. Skink wiggled his pink tail and rose on his hind legs. "I have nowhere else to live," he said. "I fear I am the last pink-tailed skink."

"Surely not," cried Gull. "It cannot be." It is true that Gull was silly, but smart enough to be a gull, and she had never known a time when someone or something was not in charge.

"It can be," said Skink. "I'm thinking of rousing Turtle." At this, the others - even Wave - became silent and fell back to watch Sun tuck himself behind Piney Point for the night. Stars began to prick the sky and look down on them.

"What does Skink mean?" asked Spider, who was not social, and apart from spinning sticky string to catch things, did not concern herself with much as long as there was something to eat.

"I will tell you," said Skink.

The moon rose and silvered and Skink saw that many of the others, especially the young ones, were looking at him, so great their love for story, and he remembered that not all creatures had been around as long as he. Mullet splashed in circles and even Horseshoe Crab crawled up on the beach and seemed to listen, though who could tell with a horseshoe crab?

Skink began to speak: "At the beginning there was the Turtle and the Stars – the very ones you see now." The creatures looked up and, seeing the stars, nodded. "Turtle swam through the stars for a long time, longer than any time you can think of, and he grew tired, for even Turtle cannot go on forever and must rest. But there was nowhere to rest, for the stars are burning things and else had not yet been made."

"Then how do you know this?" asked Cat.

"Because Turtle told me," said Skink. "Now go back to licking your bottom and listen," he said, and that is what Cat did.

"At last the stars felt sorry for Turtle, though they liked having him swim among them. 'We have made a place for you,' they said, and they told Turtle where it was – a little ball tucked into the corner of everything. So Turtle swam to the little ball, to where we are now... to World."

All the creatures looked down and some stamped their feet, if they had any.

"And because Turtle was very tired, he buried himself in the soil of the earth and went to sleep. Of course, over time Ocean rose and fell and moved things and Turtle became quite covered with mud, until at last, only his back and feet were above water. Then these too, were covered by sand and dirt and all manner of living things."

"And that is where we are now," said one of the fiddler crabs, who loved to be on - and even in - the beach.

"Exactly," said Skink. "These islands are the back and claws of Turtle, who has been sleeping all these years - though I'm thinking of waking him." Only Skink could wake Turtle.

Mullet splashed and lifted his head out of the little waves. "And what then?" he asked.

Skink was quiet for a moment. "I don't know. It has never been done. But I am the only one who can do it."

As we have said, Skink was in charge, and even Cat did not argue this. "So, I suppose," continued Skink, "that I should waken Turtle before I am gone forever, before my pink tail flicks no more."

It was now fully night and Sun had pulled in his fiery train. The salt-scented air kissed over the creatures, freshening the ones that lived by night; soporific to the ones that lived by day. Wave lapped gently upon herself as Tide turned and Ocean began to flee across the world.

"Therefore," said Skink. "I will wake Turtle ... unless ..."

"Unless?" asked the assembled (not Horseshoe Crab; it was very difficult for him to talk . . . but there are strengths other than talking).

"Unless I find a mate and a place for her eggs, I will wake Turtle."

At this, all the creatures quickly agreed to spread the word and help Skink find a mate and a place to live, for none of them wanted Turtle awakened, not being sure what that meant. They had grown used to things the way they were, even if things were no longer the way they were. And so began the great hunt.

They looked everywhere, for creatures are good at finding things if they really want to. They searched in and under houses, on the beaches, amongst the sawgrass, between rocks and under fallen trees. The water creatures swam to other islands – North Key and Seahorse and Snake Key – and searched the shores. Birds flew inland on every island to look. Skink burrowed through miles of sand. They found nothing.

Soon, men began to notice all the activity and think the creatures crazy, touched by some madness not seen heretofore. In part, this was true, for the waking of Turtle was a serious thing. Mermaids began to appear, though no one would admit to their sightings.

The creatures even tried, as much as they were able, to talk to men. The fiddler crabs spoke to their friend Leo, who was so old by now that he understood nothing and everything. When the deer heard that Skink might wake Turtle, they stood like statues beside the roads; but men only slowed their loud riding things and never stopped to talk (though one did manage to speak with Pastor Helms, but the good man only understood part of the message). No mate was found for Skink. No place for his eggs.

As the days passed, many of the birds got so upset that they left and no one knew where they went. (They lived on Seahorse Key and disappeared one night. The birds feared Seahorse was Turtle's foot, or a ridge on its shell or some other part that might awaken.)

How pleasing it would be to tell you that, at last, a wife for Skink was found, that a place safe for eggs was discovered and that all remained as it was. But it was not to be. It is not to be.

At midsummer's eve, Skink again called all the creatures to the sand. "There's nothing else to be done," he said. In the distance, Leo could be seen stumbling down the beach, guided by the fiddlers. "I'm going to wake Turtle," he said.

The creatures snorted and hissed and made whatever sounds they usually made. Pastor Helms, reading from the book of Revelation as he sat on his porch swing, noticed an odd glow in the sky, as if the sun were backing up. Little Pete swore he saw the mermaids wink in the painting in the Poseidon bar.

When old Leo finally arrived to join the circle of creatures, of created things, Skink said softly, "Wake up, Turtle."

Skink did not shout or wave his arms or prance or dance or speak mumbo-jumbo, but spoke simply and clearly, as one who had authority. After a minute, the ground began to move. Turtle was waking and that which could be shaken was shaken and that which could not be shaken was not shaken. As the creatures watched, Seahorse Key moaned terribly and began to rise from the water and then other keys began to follow, until at the last, Way Key (which was Turtle's back) lifted into the air, and Ocean rushed in with a great roar. Except for Skink, all manner of things fell into the surging waters — trees and houses, men and possessions, skiffs and nets. Yet no creature drowned, saved either by swimming to mainland ground or clinging to flotsam until reaching shallow water. Nothing was bitten, nothing was stung. Leo clung to a floating palm tree, smiling happily as his friends - the Fiddlers - clung to his beard. Only Skink remained upon Turtle.

After a while, the great Turtle rose higher and higher, extending clawed feet, stretching his neck, feeling, testing the remembered freedom of motion, swimming in slow circles until, at last, he swam out to the waiting and silent stars and vanished. All the creatures cried in sadness. This is the sound of the wind on a cold and lonely night.

And so, Turtle and Skink Pink-Tail passed from the earth.

This saddened Skink greatly, but such is the way of things, and Turtle comforted him as best he could. The stars saw all this and took compassion upon the travelers and told Turtle where he might find a ball inhabited only by skinks, of which many were female with beautiful pink tails. This gave Skink hope.

Down on earth, the humans dried themselves off and began to do what they always did, just in a different place. The land animals moved here and there, but mostly went to live in the hammock.

Sometimes, after a rest, Turtle still swims among the stars, where he may be seen enjoying his freedom (by those who are able to see him). His friend, Skink Pink-Tail – and family – often ride upon his back.

Look up.

Bonus Story!

What is a book of stories without sex and violence? Or, in this case, an unusual twist on an old tail . . .

Violence and Sex

In a fire bush on 5th Street lives a praying mantis. She is very big, eats all manner of bugs, and the occasional hummingbird if she can catch it. When the mantis's meal gets close, perhaps wondering what she's praying about (she's praying for prey), her forelegs flash and she grabs the luckless bug. Then she kills it and eats it (not always in that order), biting it into chewy morsels or just sucking out the tasty broth. This doesn't bother her because she's just a bug too.

With the male mantis, which she also eats, the praying dodge isn't necessary. All she has to do is put a little perfume behind her sexy antennae and the male comes calling. If the female feels frisky, instead of just eating him outright . . . well . . . you know. . .

PARTY!

Sometimes she bites his head off and eats it during the party. He doesn't know or care. He's a male and has already lost his mind.

This is not a problem, as the headless male continues mating for hours, even speeding up the process. He has a mini-brain in his tail.

An old story. Life goes on.

EPILOGUE

While we look not at the things which are seen, but at the things which are not seen: for the things which are seen are temporal; but the things which are not seen are eternal. - 2 Corinthians 4:18 (KJV)

WWW With Castnet

MORE PRAISE FOR CEDAR KEY STORIES

"Writing keeps him out of my hair and out of bars."
Victoria Wadley, Wife

"Meow . . ."
Squeaky the Cat

"His stories have lots of letters. Did you know hummingbirds can't walk - they can only perch? They can sure fly, though."
Margaret (CK Resident)

Old Cedar Key Map
(Not to Scale)

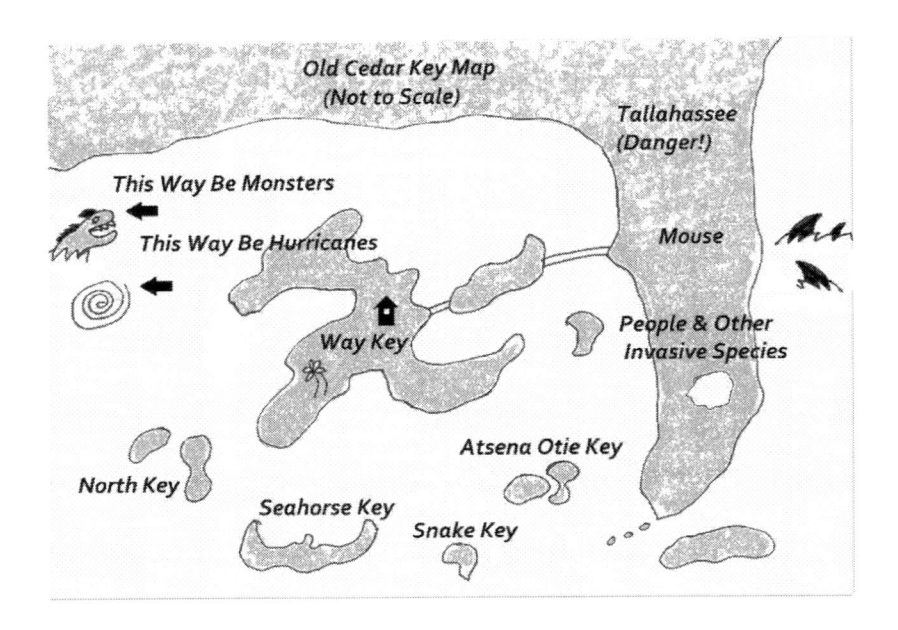

Tallahassee
(Danger!)

This Way Be Monsters

This Way Be Hurricanes

Mouse

Way Key

People & Other
Invasive Species

North Key

Atsena Otie Key

Seahorse Key Snake Key

Acknowledgement

Many thanks to my editor, Victoria Wadley, who knows way more than I ever will about this writing and English stuff. Any failures in this book are mine alone.

Also, many thanks to Rose Hamm Campbell, Anna Hodges, and Miriam Walrath Needham, for reviewing parts of this work.

ABOUT THE AUTHOR

Gary is the last Wadley that lived in the house at 4th and G Streets. He is a published poet, playwright, artist, photographer, and sometimes actor.

He is married to the lovely Vicky and has four lovely children. Everything is lovely.

Laudate Deum

You may contact him at: CedarKeyShark@gmail.com.

Made in the USA
Columbia, SC
01 December 2021